Finding Kate

A. G. Hayes

Savant Books and Publications
Honolulu, HI, USA
2016

Published in the USA by Savant Books and Publications
2630 Kapiolani Blvd #1601
Honolulu, HI 96826
http://www.savantbooksandpublications.com

Printed in the USA

Edited by Kaethe Kauffman
Cover image ID 42872116 © Tatsiana Shypulia |
Dreamstime.com
Cover Design by Daniel S. Janik

13 digit ISBN: 9780997247213

Dedication

To all my readers who enjoy the Koski and Falk stories. Truth is often hidden behind a layer of fiction, as I find in life today in many instances.

Acknowledgements

To Kaethe Kauffman, my editor, who, again, has done a terrific job. She was my compass throughout the journey.

Chapter 1

This wasn't how her week had begun.

Earlier, when Kate had finished researching the background of literary agent, Lev Leventhal, an old and trusted friend of her father, she had looked forward to meeting him. Arriving at his office on South La Cienega in Hollywood, Joanie Malone, Lev's assistant, greeted her and apologized for his absence. He was out of town at Time Was, a small hotel in the Santa Barbara Mountains, helping one of his writers suffering from writer's block, teetering on the brink of a nervous breakdown.

Naturally, Kate was disappointed, although the thought that he had gone to help a client impressed her. Joanie served coffee in the office and filled her in on her own background. Graduated from college with an MA in Information Management, she had become a temporary librarian. Two years later, she moved to Hollywood where she met Lev, who offered her a real job. She and Lev were as different as chalk and cheese. Nonetheless, within a year they had become a dynamic duo. Joanie, smart and good-looking, was superbly organized. Lev, fifty-seven, had, over the years, earned an open door to most of the top producers in town. Although he had a small stable of writers, they were all top notch. Even the young Turks recognized his Hollywood shrewdness. During their first year together, Lev discovered he also had talent as a sleuth when he single-handedly solved the murder of Cy Wald, a Hollywood mogul.

Joanie ran the office whenever Lev was out of town, and over a second cup of coffee, mentioned Lev had said the contract between the Leventhal-Malone agency and Katherine Keenan was, despite his absence, ready to sign if she was.

Kate signed right then. The thought of an agent in Hollywood who would go help a client on the verge of a breakdown cinched the deal.

Two days later, Lev Leventhal met Kate in person. He rose from behind his desk, shook hands, and indicated a well-worn leather armchair. He did not look like a sleuth who could solve a murder. Thin on top, thick around the middle, and height about five foot six, maybe eight if he stood straighter and squared his rounded shoulders.

"Sorry I was unable to be here when you came in to sign the contract; an unexpected problem." His voice was crisp, his green eyes intense. Kate instantly knew this guy could solve more than a murder.

When Lev sat back in his chair with narrowed eyes, Kate could literally feel his high hopes for her.

"Why me?" he asked.

"We met briefly when I was a student at UCLA. You said you were interested in movie technology, and I learned you are well connected in the movie industry. When I came to visit, your assistant, Joanie Malone, told me about your success as a detective, and that's something I need. Besides, my father, Ethan, always said you were someone I could trust if I needed help."

Placing her laptop on his desk, Kate sat down, smoothing the darts of her green Lyell Claire dress that showcased her unruly red hair.

Lev reddened slightly. "Thanks. Well, now that we've gotten all that out of the way, we can discuss the Frank Primo pitch."

Kate explained, "I'm ready to present my work to Mr. Primo, but I want to go over few details with you first."

"Of course, go right ahead," Lev said, his foot tapping a subtle rhythm on the floor, as if in anticipation.

Joanie's voice cut in on the intercom. "A courier is here with a package for Kate."

Perfect timing, thought Kate.

Lev snapped the intercom switch. "Bring it in."

Joanie entered carrying a small flat rectangular package and laid it on the desk. Kate smiled. "Thanks, Joanie."

Joanie left, and Kate quickly opened the package and removed a slim device about the size of an iPod. Kate attached a cable from the laptop to the device and said, "Technology will play a major role in the way this century will unfold. Computing, robotics, and biotechnology will be revolutionized."

Lev looked mystified, and nodded slowly.

Booting up her computer, Kate angled the screen toward him. "Can you see okay?"

Lev nodded.

She tapped the play button and sat back. Lev watched and heard what looked like a movie clip: A man and woman walked beside a mountain lake to soft background music. Stopping at the edge of the water, the man scooped up a flat stone and skimmed it across the lake. The girl laughed, "Not bad, three daps. Bet I can beat it!" She sorted through a few stones on the shore with the toe of her shoe until she found the right one, picked it up and sent it soaring across the lake. The screen faded to black.

"What's this?" Lev asked, his curiosity alive in his eyes.

"A clip from a computer software program I designed. I key in description, just as I would type narration in a book. However, in this case, this little box I've just attached changes what I've written into a visual scene. I describe the characters and they appear. I type dialog and the box changes it into spoken words." Looking at Lev, Kate could see he was not entirely on the same page. "Okay, picture a film script."

4

"Go on," Lev said, both feet now audibly tapping on the floor.

"When I type, instead of letters of the alphabet, my keystrokes are changed into a moving picture. Watch."

Kate typed: The man, dressed in a blue shirt and brown shorts is reading a book, sitting on a park bench. Then she clicked play and Lev immediately saw what she had typed in full color.

"As with the written word, Mr. Leventhal, when we need more detail we have to show, not tell." Lev nodded, his lips slightly parted, as if subtly panting.

Again, Kate's fingers danced across the keyboard: An elderly man dressed in a beige three-piece suit walks beside a busy highway, dazedly watching cars pass in either direction.

She glanced up at Lev. "I think I should give him a cane."

Kate keyed in: He is carrying a wooden walking stick. The picture on the screen immediately conformed to Kate's typing. Lev's body jolted in his seat.

Kate smiled at his reaction and clicked pause. "Different from anything you have ever seen, right? My software program, housed in this little side box, is unlike anything known. I direct who wears what, how they speak, move, everything. Whatever I write turns into an instant movie. This is, of course, a prototype. Later designs will include a more sophisticated dictionary of specifics to work with." Lev stared, wide-eyed, at the still frame of the old man and his stick.

"Editing, both visual and audio will be the same as polishing a draft of a typewritten script. I find that when people work with my program, they become a part of the movie. They feel it and hear it as they write. They become a part of it."

"You have a patent on this?" Lev gulped, his Adam's apple sliding up and down several times, reflecting his intense interest and rapid thoughts. "I mean, I was ready to contract with you as your agent just from what you'd said. But seeing it, however, is..."

"Yes, amazing, isn't it. That's why I want to demonstrate it to Mr. Primo. As for the patent, the US Patent and Trademark Division moves slowly. I've filed and expect a reply any day. My program also includes anti-key-login software."

Lev looked puzzled, "Key-logging? That have something to do with security?"

"Do you use a computer, Mr. Leventhal?"

"Don't even own one," he said, then paused. "Joanie has one in her office, and a laptop at home. I never got comfortable with computers; too late for me, I guess."

Kate had guessed as much and bet he did not know a Mac from a PC. "I wouldn't say that, Mr. Leventhal. Given the right introduction, I imagine you'd do fine."

"Call me Lev, Kate," he said warmly. "I didn't even learn

to type, never mind a computer. I use a cell phone, though, and I'm thinking of switching to Bluetooth."

Kate nodded, "Great. Now about key-loggin. Hackers have multiple ways at their disposal to secretly record any-one's keystrokes, and in so doing can read passwords and other private information. However, anyone attempting to hack my system will automatically destroy whatever it is they're seeking."

"How does that work?"

"I don't want to overload you with too much of the tech-nical whiz-bang. Let's just say that every time I type any-thing, it's absolutely safe."

Lev pointed at the slim piece of equipment delivered by the courier and attached to Kate's computer. "What's that?"

"That is the reason I'm able to create what I type into a moving, speaking picture. Technically speaking, it's called an interpreter program. It's what powers the base program on my computer. Both have to be connected to do what I've just demonstrated to you. You might wonder why I didn't bring it with me, but, instead, had it delivered."

"Yeah, I did."

Kate quickly detached the slim pack and pushed it across the desk to Lev. "I need a detective. I'm being watched and followed. I have no idea by whom. I never carry the two pieces together anymore. Tomorrow evening, when we meet

Mr. Primo, I want you to carry this in your inside jacket pocket. It's small. No one will know you're carrying it."

Lev began to object, but Kate held up a hand. "I will feel better if you do this. You don't mind do you?"

"Of course not, but have you spoken to the police about being followed?"

"No, I didn't want any publicity. I don't want anyone knowing what I've told and showed you."

"What you have here, Kate, is worth millions, and before our appointment with Primo, I have a lot more questions about your invention." Lev's voice quivered like a tightly strung violin string.

"I'm sure you do. Once Mr. Primo decides to use my system, all my patents are registered, and you and he sign contracts, I believe whoever is trying to steal my invention will have lost their chance."

"Let me get you a bodyguard, Kate," Lev pleaded.

"I won't need one if you just keep Al Jolson here safe. That's all I ask."

"Al Jolson?"

"When Al Jolson sang 'Mammy' in *The Jazz Singer*, he changed Hollywood overnight. My Al Jolson here is going to do the same."

Chapter 2

Lev and Kate circulated through the crowd of partygoers on stage four at Galaxy Studios in Burbank. Music blared, conversation and laughter vied with the clink of glasses. Kate turned to speak to Lev to find he was no longer at her side. As a result, Kate ended up chatting with a group of strangers standing near the band when the music suddenly stopped and producer Frank Primo, tall and elegantly dressed in an impeccable dinner jacket and black tie, stepped on stage and waved to the crowd.

"Thank you. Thank you all, but this is *your* wrap party folks."

A wrap party was a cross between a political convention and a brawl, and held at the completion of a movie. Primo ran a finger around the inside of his shirt collar, licked his lips and continued.

"I couldn't have made this picture without every one of you here, with big special kudos to our stars, Stella and Chaz."

Pushed up close to the stage, Kate saw sweat break out on Primo's temples and his knuckles whiten as he gripped the microphone stand. A spotlight jabbed down from above and enveloped Stella Rae, a young woman in her early twenties in tight, low-slung jeans and a brief top revealing a red rose tattooed on her right shoulder. High cheekbones, blonde hair cut short, spiky, and red pouty lips completed her stylish look. Next to her slouched hunk Chaz Falconer, Stella's highly publicized future husband. Chaz, with a three-day stubble and uncombed dark hair, wearing an Armani tuxedo and an open neck red shirt, smiled graciously and waved to all the little people. Each time either one of them made a movie, Stella and Chaz each made twenty million dollars. Rumor had it that after they were married, they were going to a village in China to adopt a baby girl and name her Olympia in honor of the Beijing Olympic games.

Suddenly, Primo convulsed in a paroxysm of coughing. One hand firmly gripping to the microphone, he clawed frantically at his tie, eyes widening into a terrified stare as his knees buckled and he crashed to the stage dragging the microphone with him.

Utter silence, then cries of dismay rose from the audience.

Someone turned to a security guard and grasped his arm. "Call an ambulance!" The guard pressed the send button on his shoulder-mounted two-way. "Code eight. Stage four."

Paramedics arrived and Primo made his stage exit on a gurney amid rumors that he had suffered a heart attack. Security then began ushering the crowd out of the sound stage; being close to a door, Kate was one of the first pushed out into the night.

A. G. Hayes

Chapter 3

"Hell of way to go, Lev."

Lev turned. Charles Vance stood next to him holding a glass of vodka. "Yeah, what happened?"

"Don't know, could have been anything."

Vance, in his mid-sixties and healthy, was still remembered as a star of the forties and fifties who'd sung his way to a fortune, collecting several glamorous wives along the way. He'd appeared in musicals during the Hollywood Golden Era when Astaire and Kelly danced for MGM. Now he owned a posh supper club on the Strip, Charley Vee's, and would belt out a song at the club on special occasions.

"I'm searching for Kate," Lev muttered.

"I saw her talking to a group of the A-list guests just before the ruckus." He aimed his glass in the direction of the stage.

"Thanks. I'm sure she's here someplace," Lev said

"How long has she been with your agency, Lev?"

"A week. Joanie signed her up when I was up in Santa Barbara. Kate's a great talent and I'm lucky to get her."

Vance took a sip of his vodka and said, "I hear she's a smart cookie."

Lev nodded, "Rich grandparents, too. They educated her in private schools in Switzerland and the US. She's fluent in German and French. Graduated Cum Laude from UCLA film school prior to her twentieth birthday. Her first screenplay, *Mouse Trip*, a murder mystery solved by a teen-aged computer hacker, won the Grand Jury Prize at Sundance. Her second film, *Download*, another mystery that took place in the world of hi-tech computers, and software piracy took second at Cannes."

Vance finished his drink. "Sounds like a winner. Don't worry, she's around here some place. Take care, Lev, Vicky calls." There were still a few guests standing around and talking while security was busy ordering them to leave.

Lev took a quick circuit of the cavernous sound stage but it proved fruitless. Kate was gone. He stepped outside, knowing that Charlie Vance's longevity in Hollywood was partly due to his being a master bullshitter, and the rest due to his latest trophy wife, Vicky Vance, a syndicated newspaper columnist, always ready to crank out the latest celebrity news including inside dirt on Hollywood scandals. Vicky had a weekend TV show that could churn out more gossip in ten minutes than Oprah could in one hour. Vicky carried influence in town.

Lev was almost to his car when he remembered Kate always carried a cell phone with her. Luckily, he'd entered her number on his phone's list.

Her cell rang ten times; it didn't even switch to call forwarding. Something was wrong. She normally picked up a call on the second ring.

He called her home phone and left a message on her answering machine.

Driving out the studio main gate, he decided to go to her place and check things out. His intuition told him to be extra cautious, especially after what Kate had said about being followed. Turning left onto Barham Boulevard, he headed toward the Hollywood Freeway.

It was after eleven when he pulled into her driveway noting there were no lights on in the single story stucco house. Lev rang the doorbell and heard an "Avon Calling" chime. He waited, then headed down the driveway and checked the back door. It was unlocked. No one left a door unlocked in Hollywood, especially at this time of the night. *Was it left unlocked on purpose or had someone unlocked it and entered?* he wondered.

He should call the cops, but there was no guarantee they'd show up simply because of an open back door.

That shifted Lev's paranoia into overdrive. She could be lying in a pool of blood somewhere in the house. Hurrying back up the driveway to his car, Lev grabbed a flashlight from under the front seat, returned to the kitchen door and slowly pushed it open. He remained motionless for a few seconds, scarcely breathing. There was not a sound in the house.

Snapping on the flashlight, he bounced the beam around the kitchen and cautiously headed toward the front of the two-bedroom, one-bath home. It didn't take long to assure himself that Kate was not slumped unconscious in the living room. In fact, nothing at all seemed to have been disturbed.

He made his way down the hall to Kate's home office, opened the door and snapped on the light switch. *What a mess!* his mind screamed. Books and papers were scattered all across the floor. A computer desk held no computer. A three-drawer file had all three drawers open; two drawers were empty. Not only was Kate missing, so was a hunk of her home office.

Lev made an anonymous call to the cops, reporting a break in at 933 N. Sweetzer, then, moving fast, returned to his car and headed home.

He should have waited for the police, but he was in no mood to go through the usual Q and A procedure. He was too worn out. He needed time to think and if possible, grab some sleep.

His dash clock showed one fifty a.m. as Lev turned off the ignition, locked the car and entered his place on Lookout Mountain Avenue. His house was located in a tangle of twisting roads and lanes that twined through the hills above West Hollywood.

Lev and his sister had grown up in this very house. She'd married a patent lawyer a year after she completed college, and now lived in Florida with two kids. Their parents had long since passed and he'd inherited the house. The rambling redwood with a huge outdoor deck perched on stilts cantilevered deeply into the side of a ravine overlooked the lights of an ever-growing Hollywood.

The quietness of the hills was always a welcome solace after the intense hustle and bustle of Hollywood. Despite his tiredness, he took time to listen to the silence, something he found himself doing increasingly these days. He opened the fridge, grabbed a Bud, headed out to the deck and slumped into an old Adirondack chair, pulled the tab and took a deep swig as the distant howl of a coyote floated on the night breeze. Given half a chance, life could be sweet.

A. G. Hayes

Chapter 4

Amid the jostling crowd outside the sound stage, Kate suddenly felt a hand grip her arm and heard aman's gruff voice ordering her to go with him. She pulled back, but he already had her in the shadows. "Kate, come with me. Right now. You're in danger." She twisted back and saw it was a security guard, tall and intent, his eyes full of urgency. "Frank Primo was murdered. You could be next. Come with me."

The shock of what he'd said temporarily stopped any further resistance, and Kate was pulled deeper into the darkness. By now, most of the crowd had left the building and were some distance ahead, streaming towards the main gate.

He yanked her to the side towards the blackness of the studio back lot. It was then Kate knew something was wrong. She tried to pull away and took a swing at him, but he moved too fast and kicked her Sergio Rossi's out from under her until she was face down on the asphalt.

"Bitch," he grunted, pulling her arms behind her back and snapping on a pair of cuffs. "Do as I tell you next time."

Kate tried to lift her head and scream. But, sprawled face down, all she could do was suck grit and dust.

She felt him push up the sleeve of her jacket, and

twitched at the jab of a needle into her arm. Immediately, she felt a sliding, sinking sensation as if her entire body was slowly soaking into the earth, while a voice, far away, repeatedly told her to relax.

The next she knew, she was on her back on a canvas cot with the mother of all hangovers. Trying to open her eyes was a chore. Her head thumped like an uneven load in a washing machine. She tried to move her hands and found them still handcuffed beneath her back.

As Kate struggled to focus, the same security guard leaned over her, his breath reeking of stale fast food. Quickly, she snapped her eyes shut.

"Can't fool me, Kate, I know you're awake. You're a missing person and only I know where you are."

Think! her brain screamed. Kate Keenan had written hundreds of scenes like this. She knew about bad guys, from chain saw murderers to clowns who bury their victims under the house. Slowly, she opened an eye."Where the hell am I?" she asked.

"You're a writer, Kate; you know the best villains would never answer that question. And I'm top of the line," he said, smirking at his joke.

"Take off the manacles and I promise to listen up. They're so tight they might have already done permanent damage to these fingers I depend on for my living."

A flicker in his eyes told her that, for some reason, her hands mattered to him. He flipped Kate over like a hamburger and unlocked the cuffs. Her hands were numb and she rubbed them hard to get the circulation moving. Then she sat up, eyes darting around the cell-like cinderblock room with its single light bulb dangling from the ceiling. Where was her laptop? Kate had carried it with her to the wrap party, slung across her shoulders for safety. Her skin tingled with the realization and panic it was nowhere in sight.

"You stole my computer, you son of a bitch!" Kate yelled. The security man leaned against the wall and watched her. "It's safe. It's not going any place. I'm being paid to look after you and your gear."

The last buzz from whatever he'd stuck in her arm was starting to wear off and she was beginning to feel almost normal. "Why the hell did you drug me? And what on earth for?"

"Your own safety," he drawled.

"From what?" Kate asked rubbing her still sore hands. "You're not the safest person I've ever met."

Opening the door of the concrete room, he stepped aside and signaled with an upturned hand. "C'mon, I'll show you your office where you'll be working until your assignment is complete."

Kate crossed to the door and into a larger, rectangular

room with the lingering musty smell of an unused cellar. Three parallel metal racks standing over six feet tall ran off into the darkness. A light abruptly clicked on in the distant corner, followed by another immediately above a large wooden desk located ten feet in front of her. On it was her laptop. She noted a bright yellow cable snaking from the darkness plugged into the side of the computer.

"Just like at home, Kate. No one to disturb you," the skinny man purred. "Controlled air temperature year round— a writers, or in your immediate case, a programmer's dream."

Kate turned and looked across at her keeper lolling against row after row of film canisters stacked on the metal shelves, and asked, "What assignment?"

"You'll know soon enough," and asked if she'd ever been in a film vault before. With the realization, Kate felt a tightness grip her chest. She was underground! She began to breathe fast and shallow, the word "vault" conjuring up a place of darkness, doom and death. Seeing her reaction, he again assured her that her safety was his responsibility. No one knew she was here except himself and the person who'd hired him.

Kate slumped into the ergonomically correct office chair in front of the desk and stared vacantly at her silent laptop.

"And if I need something in order to finish this 'assignment'?" Kate asked.

"Anything you require will be provided. By me. You just have to ask." The man pointed to the yellow cable indicating it was her only connection to the outside world.

"Access to the internet?" she asked, already knowing the answer.

"Kate, Kate, Kate," the man replied shaking his head from side to side. "Please don't underestimate me or the man I work for. All possible access to the world, outside of this single cable, have been blocked. As to any further requests, I can only assure you that I will provide you with anything you need to complete your assignment. Anything within reason."

So, she was a prisoner in a film vault. Less than an hour ago, she'd been with her agent at a wrap party, waiting to show Frank Primo her revolutionary program. Everything was going great until the man collapsed. If she'd just been able to find Lev before this creep grabbed her, she wouldn't be in this mess.

A. G. Hayes

Chapter 5

The distant but incessant ringing of the house phone awakened Lev with a start. Night was already shifting to day, the sky tinging with the orange streaks of dawn.

Hauling himself awkwardly from the hard wooden deck chair, he stumbled into the house and snapped on the kitchen light. The phone quit ringing. The microwave clock broadcast six a.m. in light-blue digital numbers.

He didn't usually fall asleep on the deck; he'd been worn out last night. Then he remembered Kate. Damn! That could have been her calling! There was no message, so he dialed her home number. Her answering machine eventually told him to leave a message.

He showered, shaved, and ate a fried banana sandwich and was on his third cup of coffee when the phone rang again. Scooping it up before the second ring, he rasped, "Hello, Kate?"

"No. It's me, Joanie. What's with your voice?" Before he could answer, she continued, "I'm at the office. I came in early to finish some work and I found an envelope stuffed under the door."

Envelopes stuffed beneath doors never bode good news.

"Read it to me," he growled.

"Okay. 'Kate will contact you soon'."

"That's it? Nothing else?"

"No, except the letters of each word were cut out of a magazine or a newspaper, you know, like a ransom note."

Lev choked, "Cut out letters? Ransom note?"

"That's why I called at once, Lev."

Chapter 6

"It's on my desk." Joanie Malone handed her boss a mug of Grand Marnier-laced coffee, her standard sedative for his nervous tension attacks.

Lev accepted the cup and took a long draught as he studied the pasted words.

"Holy shit! She's been kidnapped!" he again concluded.

"The note says Kate will contact you soon. It doesn't say she's been kidnapped, Lev."

"A note spelled out in newspaper clippings and pushed under our front door sometime in the night doesn't smack of a social letter, Joanie."

"There's nothing mentioned about a ransom."

He signaled for another ration of brandy. "And yet…"

"You're going to call the cops?

"Calling the cops could compromise Kate's safety. I need to think. In the meantime, get me the list of the 'A' group at last night's wrap party."

Joanie tipped some more Grand Marnier into his mug and left. She returned with the list and laid it on his desk. "There were nine people on the 'A' list."

Lev scanned the names: Charles and Vicky Vance, Stella

Rae, Chaz Falconer, Pattie Primo, Don Ames, Franz Villand, Stacy Hart, and Hank Tolomeo. He knew all of them personally except Franz Villand and Hank Tolomeo. He'd heard Villand's name sometime in the past. Tolomeo's name had been in 'Varity' several times the last few months concerning his hi-tech computer company, TolomeoTechnics.

Lev ordered Joanie to get Charles Vance, the celebrity nightclub owner, on the phone. Three minutes later Lev was listening to his booming voice resounding in his ear.

"Hell of wrap party, don't you think, Lev? Primo went out in style."

"I'm not calling about Primo."

"Vicky's been swamped with calls from around the country trying to find out what happened."

"What do you mean? I thought Primo died of a heart attack."

"Word around town is someone might have arranged for his heart to stop."

"Murder?" Lev whispered.

"Yeah, I thought that's what you were calling about."

"No, I was calling to ask about Kate. I still haven't heard from her, and I recall you with her at the party."

"Yeah, she was talking with me, Stacy Hart and Stella Rae as Primo came on stage."

"Did you see her after Primo keeled over?"

"No, like everyone, my attention was on the stage. You think Kate was involved?"

"Involved? You mean because of what she might have seen? Or something about the way he died?"

Charles hesitated. "Well, from what you're telling me, she seems to have vanished, so. It could be either. Have you called the cops?"

"Spoke to them last night." This wasn't a lie. He'd called about the break-in to Kate's place on Sweetzer.

"Well, that's about all you can do, Lev."

"I'm planning on questioning various people who were at the party. Someone might be able to tell me something."

"I'd leave that to the cops if I were you."

"It's not about it being a possible homicide, Charles. I need to find my missing client. Don't you understand?"

"Of course I do, Lev, and I'll do all I can to help." Clearing his throat, he continued, "You might want to start with Stacy Hart."

"Thanks, Charles, I'll do that. Talk to you later."

Lev tilted back in his chair and stared at the ceiling. What was he getting into? He'd known Stacy Hart for years; she was highly respected in both Hollywood and New York. She owned a press agency which represented many of the top names in publishing and show business. What Charles' or his nosey wife, Vicky, might not know, Stacy would.

He pressed the button on his intercom.

"Joanie, get Stacy Hart on the line, please."

Chapter 7

Joanie's voice came over the intercom: "Stacy Hart on three."

"Thanks, Joanie. Stace, can you make lunch? It's important."

"What's up?"

He brought her quickly up to date about Kate.

"You think she's been abducted?"

Who else but Stace would jump to using a word like that in this town? "I don't know. There's certainly a possibility, but I can't think why."

"Right, you can buy me lunch at the Polo Lounge. Shall we say one?"

"One. See you there."

The Beverly Hills Hotel was an oasis amidst palms and splendid flower gardens that bloomed and blossomed year round. Lev drove up the curving driveway toward the imposing pink building that for so many years has been the cradle of luxury to the rich, famous and notorious.

Stace, already seated, was sipping a tall drink; Lev knew it was not iced tea. She reminded him of a quote he'd once heard: "Taking joy in life is a woman's best cosmetic." Stace was a woman with a brilliant business mind, matched with striking beauty. Not yet forty, her two publicity offices, one in New York City, the other in Beverly Hills, were in constant demand.

"Am I late?" Lev pulled out a chair.

Stacy smiled. "Fashionably so. Now what's all this about Kate vanishing?"

Before he could answer, a waiter appeared at the table to take his order. "Give me one of those," Lev said, indicating Stacy's drink.

"I'll have another and the McCarthy salad," Stacy added.

"Make it two salads." Lev announced as he shook out the pink linen napkin and placed it across his knees. "Charles Vance said you and Stella Rae were talking with Kate when Primo made his grand entrance.

"He's correct. Kate was standing right between us. We all turned toward the stage at the same time."

"Was she still with you after Primo collapsed?"

Stace looked deep into her drink before answering. "When that happened everything went wild. I'm not sure."

"Did you recall seeing her after the medics arrived?"

"No. I remember Stella talking with Chaz." She paused. "To be honest, Lev, I don't know where she went."

What he was hearing was so far not worth the price of lunch at the Lounge.

"Wait a minute!" Stace exclaimed. "I do remember something."

The waiter returned with the drinks and salads. Lev leaned forward eagerly as the waiter left and Stacy continued. "Franz Villand, the actor, and Don Ames, the writer. I recall them standing by an exit talking to Kate. Next time I looked, all three were gone."

Two writers and a latter day Lon Chaney had mysteriously vanished from the scene, he thought. Taking a long sip of his drink, Lev asked, "I've met Don Ames, but I only know of Villand. Villand was the 'Man of a Thousand Faces', right?"

Stace nodded. "Right, but he's not done much work the last few years."

"Ran out of faces?"

"I guess. Today, computer graphics do a better job without having to carry workman's comp."

"I think I may have seen Hank Tolomeo at the party," he ventured.

Stace sighed. "So did a lot of people who wished he'd never been born."

"What do you mean?"

"You're kidding, Lev. TolomeoTecnics has been impacting the entire movie industry with its increasingly sophisticated robots Frank Primo had told Hank Tolomeo he might consider using TolomeoTecnics robots in place of stunt actors in his next production. They were this close to a deal. If the deal went through, many thought the impact on the movie industry would be greater than the introduction of sound." She held her thumb and forefinger almost touching each other.

"What is it exactly about this kind of technology that has the town so rattled?" The incredibly realistic scene of the couple walking besides a lake that Kate had produced for him in the office flashed across his mind.

"Wish I knew for sure. I've heard rumors that the right technology could save producers a ton of money and put a lot of people in the industry out of work. Not even Vicky Vance and her spies have found out what's going on, but whatever it is, it's big."

"We've both seen new production systems impact Holly-wood, Stace: Cinemascope, Three-D, Wide-Screen, I-Max. All were similarly hyped, but in the end, they've ended up requiring more people and money."

She patted her lips with a tip of her napkin. "All I know for sure is that TolomeoTechnics was betting all their savings on Primo using their system. It was to be TT's big showcase for the industry worldwide. People like Franz Villand should be happy Primo's gone."

Lev nodded. "Meaning the longer computerized productions and imagery are kept out of film, the better the chance for actors like him, right?"

"Yes, also many special effects companies, production companies, and stunt persons would find themselves out of business." Stace shook her head, "Hollywood without real live actors, videographers, gaffers, makeup artists, scene builders…" Stacy's voice trailed off as she skewered a piece of tomato. "If and when that happens, Lev, *we* could be in the same boat."

The lunch proved a bummer. Bad news. No leads. Talk about doom and gloom. Lev pushed his plate aside. "You really think it'll happen, Stace?"

"Not overnight I don't, but think about it: What if it were possible to make and show movies without the cost of stars, supporting actors, backups, stand-ins, extras, and all the various trades, guilds and unions that go into making a feature. Perhaps I should take on TT as one of my clients."

Lev switched the conversation. "Any idea where I can find Franz Villand? He might have a lead on where Kate went after they left the sound stage."

"No; however, you said Villand, Ames and Kate were together. You know Don Ames well and he's quite approachable. How about trying him?" Stacy asked.

"I turned down one of his scripts once, and he's never forgotten. He bad-mouths me every opportunity he gets. He hates my guts," Lev admitted.

"Then call Vicky Vance. If anyone, she'd knows how to find Villand."

On that positive note, they switched to ice cream, coffee and gossip.

On the way back, traffic on Sunset was, as usual, at a crawl. Lev figured Stace would have called Vicky Vance by now and word would be out that Kate was missing, just as he'd planned. Their tête-à-tête had also helped Lev identify another place to start in his search.

Driving past the UCLA campus, his mind returned to the days when Kate was still a student there in theater arts. He had been asked to address her class and remembered her vocally emphasizing the future importance of having a platform in which one could create moving images constructed digitally to simulate imagined realities. While others continued to talk about it, she had gone ahead and done it. Later, when she approached him as her agent, he didn't have the chance to go into details with her, or for the two of them to present her system to Primo. After talking to Stacy about TolomeoTechnics, could it be possible Kate had been spirited away because of her new technology? Or, was someone attempting to steal Kate's program to sell it to TolomeoTechnics? If he understood what she'd said correctly, her program wouldn't work without the part nicknamed Al Jolson, that he carried in his pocket. If someone abducted Kate or stole her program, how long would it take the thief to figure out her agent had the missing piece of the puzzle?

A. G. Hayes

Chapter 8

The first thing Lev heard as he entered his office was Joanie's animated voice. "You didn't turn on your cell, did you? You left it off, and I couldn't get hold of you."

"What happened?" The way the day was going, he wasn't sure he really wanted to know.

"A friend of Kate's called. He wants to talk to you."

He definitely wanted to know more about this. "Phone lines run all the way to the Polo Lounge, Joanie. What did you tell him?"

"To hoof it over here. He sounded upset."

"Good girl. In the meantime, get Vicky Vance on the line." Lev walked into his office and closed the door. A moment later, he was on the line with Vicious Vicky.

"Lev, darling, how nice of you to call," Vicky drawled. "What juicy morsel you have for me?"

"Actually, Vicky I'm seeking, not giving."

"Oh, you wonderful man. Didn't I see you at last night's catastrophe?"

"I saw you there, but, as usual, you were busy and I didn't want to butt in."

"Silly boy," she cooed. "I would have loved to chat

awhile with you. What is it you seek?"

"I need to talk with Franz Villand."

"Franz! What has that recluse done now?"

"Well, nothing as far as I know. I just wanted to ask him a couple of questions."

"Is it about what happened last night to poor Primo?" At least she mentioned the deceased.

"No, not about 'poor Primo'. I wonder if you knew where I could contact Villand." He had no doubt that by now, Stace had told her he was searching for Kate.

"Well, I could put out feelers for you. We have to work together in this town, don't we, Lev?" which was columnist code for, you scratch my back and I'll scratch yours.

"Vicky," Lev replied softly. "Do it and I'll owe you."

"Yes, yes, you will, dear Lev. Give me your cell number. I may have to call you at an odd time. Never know in our business, do we?"

Lev gave her his cellular number. "Call any time, Vicky. I'll be available."

"Call me anytime, too, Lev. Ta-ta."

Lev was glad the fencing match with Vicky Vance, wife of Charles Vance, the owner of Charley Vee's, was over. In one short afternoon, he'd had to come into close contact with a press agent and a gossip columnist deluxe. He squirmed, fully aware he'd have to pay dearly for each later. There were no freebies in Hollywood.

Leaning back, he replayed the dramatic end of the wrap party in his mind. Stace said Kate had been standing next to the exit with Ames and Villand. Until Lev located Villand and listened to his version of what happened, he was stuck on square one. He pulled the 'A' list toward him and put check marks next to Vicky Vance, Stacy Hart, and Charles Vance.

A. G. Hayes

Chapter 9

Joanie announced over the intercom, "Kate's 'friend' is here. Shall I send him in?"

"Yes, of course," replied Lev.

There was a light tap on the door before it opened, revealing a dark haired man in his mid-twenties peeping in.

"I had to come see you, Mr. Leventhal."

"Come in. Sit down." Lev indicated the comfortable client chair. The young man smiled and folded his slim form into the well-worn leather seat. Legs crossed, he leaned back and quickly scanned the cluttered, untidy office, and then stared at Lev with deep brown eyes. "Kate gave me your number," he said, "in case anything happened. My name is Melhi Pashagora. Kate and I went to UCLA together. We were classmates."

Lev felt a surge of adrenalin. "Exactly what do you mean, 'if anything happens'?"

"She told me she had a feeling she was being followed. It was one reason she said she wanted to meet you."

"When was this?"

"Last week. I asked her to call me and check in every day. I called her house and cell phone the last two days with no answer. I'm worried, Mr. Leventhal. I notified the police but was told they don't consider anyone a missing person until seventy-two hours have passed."

"When exactly did you contact them?"

"This morning. Then I called your office."

Here was someone who'd spent four years with Kate at UCLA. The young man could be a big help.

"Did you both study film writing at UCLA?"

"Yes, we used to compete with each other, in a friendly way, of course." He smiled, as if talking about Kate made him feel better.

Lev nodded. "Kate also studied computing in film and the arts, right?"

"We both did. TFT—Theater, Film and Television. They used to call us the Competing Computerites."

"Are you a working writer now, Mr. Pashagora?"

"Not in the literal sense. And please, call me Mel, everyone does." He took a deep breath then continued. "After graduation, Apple recruited me, and now I write software and work closely with the digital environment platform group Apple runs in conjunction with UCLA."

"Sounds like an important position, Mel."

"It is, and like Apple says, 'the importance of having a platform in which one can create moving images that are artificially constructed to simulate imagined realities cannot be overestimated'. Apple firmly believes it will increasingly become the basis for all art forms in the future.'"

"You sound very sincere."

"I am. And it's the reason I'm deeply concerned about Kate's disappearance."

"What do you mean?"

Mel glanced at his hands clenched firmly together on his lap. "It all began two days before we graduated. It was late and we were the only two left in the 'Bull Pen,' a nickname for an area of the lab that students have access to twenty-four/seven. It was two fifty-eight a.m. I recall the exact time, I still have the digital copy I made of a test she had run.

"What sort of test?" Lev asked.

"Kate had designed a radical piece of software and wanted me to see it. We were both jazzed with the results."

"Tell me about it," Lev said. Mel hesitated, but his concern for Kate was stronger than his reticence to share about the program.

"I must first ask you one thing, Mr. Leventhal. What I'm about to reveal could well be tied to her disappearance and be detrimental to her ever being found alive. You must agree not repeat what I'm about to tell you to anyone. Anyone, understand?"

"You have my word, Mel. I also want to find Kate," Lev replied in all earnestness.

"Thank you." Mel chewed his bottom lip for a second. "What would you say if I were to tell you that it is possible to create movie action on the big screen just by typing in dialog and description as one would do when writing any normal script? With her new program, instead of type, the actual movie activity appears on screen." A faint smile crossed the young man's face. "John Landis, the famous movie director, always said if Hollywood could find a way to make a movie without a director they would. Well, Kate has. Without a director, producer, actors, supporting staff, background, sound, you name it."

Lev leaned forward and said softly, "Kate gave me a demonstration of this program, here in my office." He didn't reveal that Kate had contracted with him to be her agent and had left a crucial part of the equipment with him.

Mel stiffened visibly. "Why would she do that?"

"We were to meet with Frank Primo after the wrap party for his latest film. He had let it be known to the movie community of his interest in doing a technologically innovative film next. Unfortunately, Primo died before we could meet with him and demonstrate Kate's system. Who else knows about this system?"

"No one as far as I know. Kate made me promise to keep it quiet because we knew her discovery would change Hollywood filmmaking forever. She alone knows the actual construction design of the program. I only saw it work, as you apparently did," Mel said.

"Could someone have picked up on her test from the Bull Pen?" Lev asked.

"It's possible, I suppose, although she kept the details strictly to herself," Mel replied.

"What about hackers? There must have been some in the class," Lev inquired.

"Kate and I are good enough programmers to know how to prevent the best hackers from breaking into her computer or program. Towards the end, she announced she had built in several 'safeguards' which she never shared with me. In the end, we were both recruited by top companies. I had to decide between joining the FBI computer fraud division and Apple after graduation." Mel said, unabashed.

"And Kate decided to continue writing screenplays while continuing to advance her computerized movie production system?" Lev offered.

"Not exactly. The National Security Agency approached her and would have taken her in a moment. She told them she'd seriously think about, while she finished a couple of films," Mel said.

"Sundance and Cannes, right?" Lev asked.

"Yes." Mel appeared increasingly uncomfortable with Lev's surprising knowledge of Kate and her program. "She's a very determined woman, Mr. Leventhal. She takes after her father, Ethan."

Lev raised his eyebrows. "Meaning?"

"Ethan Keenan, was a screenwriter here Hollywood some twenty years ago. He suffered a breakdown after his wife's death, took to drinking, and eventually abandoned Kate. She was reared by her grandparents—rich grandparents, who made sure she had the best education possible. She grew up believing her father was dead. It was not until her third year at UCLA that she discovered he was still alive."

For Lev, the disappearance of Kate was taking on a de-cidedly different tone. He clearly needed to learn more about the relationship between Kate and this young man. Lev wondered about NSA. If they wanted her to work for them, they likely knew about her program and it's implications beyond Hollywood. Now reported missing person, Lev speculated whether NSA might also be attempting locate her. Or were they perhaps involved in her disappearance?

Chapter 10

Her scumbag security guard had been gone for almost two hours leaving Kate plenty of time to scrutinize every inch of her prison. The film vault smelled of acid and aging rubbish. Workbenches lined three of the four walls. The benches, unlike the rows of film canisters stacked neatly on the metal shelves, were heaped with bent film reels, some containing deteriorating celluloid film. Old newspapers and tin cans were scattered about the cement floor.

A dingy bathroom with a rust-stained washbasin and a mirror of flyblown glass was located down a short hallway off the main vault area. Kate pulled a couple of pieces of toilet paper from a half-filled roll and wiped the mirror. Her reflection was not complimentary. Her hair was a tangled mess. Dirt streaked down one side of her face. Her diamond earring had disappeared from her left earlobe. The hot water faucet refused to budge, and when struck repeatedly, groaned and vibrated as she cranked it until a trickle of cold water begrudgingly dribbled into the grimy bowl. Kate removed the other stud, tucked it into her pocket and attempted a wash and brush up.

A second reconnaissance of her prison, revealed that the

only exit the film vault to the outside was the solid metal door her captor had gone out of a couple of hours ago. She toyed briefly with the idea of trying to hide and overpower her jailer when he returned with food, but decided brain over brawn was a better plan. She'd wait and see how things went when he got back.

Returning to the desk, Kate slumped wearily into the chair and turned on her computer. It booted up, displaying the expected screen saver of Mount Lee, only now it had the Hollywood sign superimposed on it within a red circle with a black line running diagonally through it. Below that were three new word-buttons: "Welcome," "Notes" and "Menu." Someone had been tampering with her computer, but hadn't attempted to hack into the movie production program. Had they tried the latter, her computer would have been a pool of melted metal and plastic. It was one of several safeguards Kate had added before appealing to Lev for help. Kate clicked on "Welcome."

Her computer screen went blank for a moment, and then some text appeared as if being typed on a distant typewriter: "I will visit you soon. It will be beneficial for us to meet in person."

Kate next opened "Notes." This time the computer responded: "Leave notes, we will go over them tomorrow."

Who is this nut? Kate cursed silently.

"Menu," when clicked, simply resulted in: "To be filled in before eight o'clock in the morning each day."

Clearly, Kate's computer was directly linked to another by way of the yellow cable. That meant that even if there was a way to send a message, her abductor and likely her service guard would immediately know. Kate clicked on Notes and, ignoring the previous response, typed, "I quit playing games in the eighth grade." Then she switched off her computer and glared at the screen, her mind screaming, *Where are Mel and Lev when I need them?*

A. G. Hayes

Chapter 11

Before his next meeting with Mel, Lev had discrete inquiries made into the man's background, and discovered Mel was Kate's fiancé. Furthermore, the two appeared to be keeping the fact a secret from his father, Kumar Pashagora, owner of the largest film production studio in India. Bollywood already out-produced the rest the world and if they got hold of Kate's program, they could easily monopolize the world entertainment market.

As agreed, Mel stopped by Lev's office late the next afternoon and Lev immediately launched into the questions he'd been stewing over.

"Why did you remain in the U.S. after graduation? Surely, your father could have used your expertise," Lev began.

"Yes, of course." Mel's eyebrows arched, making his eyes widen as if he hadn't expected the question. "Kate and I were...well...secretly engaged to be married, and I wanted us to be married *before* returning home. My family, Lev, has many long held traditions. They'd never permit me to be married outside of the family religion."

"So what would happen when you returned to India with

an American wife?"

Mel shrugged, "Kate and I agreed we'd cross that bridge when we came to it. For now, all I want to do is to find my fiancé."

Lev swigged the remains of the coffee Joanie had served before leaving for the day. He decided not to ask any further questions, and instead, urge the young man to talk while observing him closely.

Mel, obviously uncomfortable with what he'd just disclosed, asked, "So the next person on your list is Villand, the Man with a Thousand Faces?"

"Yes, I'm waiting for a call as to where I can find him." Lev had no sooner spoken, than his cellphone rang. It was Vicky Vance. Lev tapped it onto speaker and nodded to Mel.

"See, dear boy? I said I'd get back to you. Now, about Villand. I could compose an entire column on his goings on but it wouldn't interest most of today's readers. Not spicy enough. He's just another washed up actor. A nobody."

"He made it to the wrap party, Vicky."

"So did many other nobodies, Lev. He was there in the hope of sniffing out a walk-on in poor Primo's next picture. He and Don Ames…"

"Don Ames? That creep had nothing to do with Primo's next picture. It was going to be Kate's film."

"Ah, so right, dear boy. I'm told that Ames was very unhappy when Primo turned him down. My spies report both he and Villand saying how they hoped something would occur to stop the picture going into production."

"Who heard them?"

"Can't say," Vicky said quickly. "But I trust my sources."

"So where do I find Frank Villand?"

"North Hollywood, an area east of Vineland, houses and commercial buildings mixed together. Fourty-five-thirty-one Sherman Court. He arrived home a short time ago."

"Thanks Vicky, I owe you."

"Of course you do, silly boy. So stay in touch, especially if you find something I should know."

"You'll be the first, Vicky. Ta-Ta."

Lev raised his eyebrows and shrugged. "That, Mel, was Vicious Vicky, the gossip columnist. Now I know where to find Villand."

"I'd like to go with you," Mel stated quickly. "If it's okay." Villand's address was a twenty-minute drive via Laurel Canyon. 4531 Sherman Court turned out to be a scruffy yellow stucco house that had been through too many earthquakes, and had not received enough aid from FEMA. Pulling to the curb, they stared at the forlorn residence.

"Wow. It's hard to believe this guy was once a big name in movies," Mel whispered.

"That's show biz. Let's pay him a visit."

A rusted alternating convex and concave galvanized metal tapestry of neglect that once had been a four-foot cyclone fence sagged around the property. Lev had to push hard to open the gate, causing it to scrape on the cracked concrete pathway. He rang the doorbell, no answer. He rapped on the front door and waited.

"Maybe he's not home," Mel began.

Lev held a finger to his lips. "Wait." Finally, the front door creaked open about half an inch.

"If you're selling, I'm not buying. If you're preaching, I'm not a believer."

"My name is Lev Leventhal, I'm an agent."

The door opened another inch, and one of Frank Villand's thousand faces peered out. This one was pinched, gray and wrinkled.

"What kind of agent?"

"Theatrical." The door swung wide enough for them to see a jockey-sized man in his underwear and carpet slippers.

"Hey! You're the guy who helped solve the murders in Santa Barbara, right?"

This was the last thing Lev expected, but before he could answer, Villand continued. "Read about it in *Varity*. My pal says you're a prick."

"Thanks. I'd like to ask you a couple of questions."

"Don Ames, that's the guy who said it," Villand offered.

An overpowering smell of stale cigarette smoke wafted from within the house. "Well, yeah, he would," Lev said. "We had a falling out. Can we come in?"

"Who's he?" Villand pointed a thin, furrowed finger.

"A friend of mine," Lev said.

"He looks like vice to me."

Mel stepped closer. "I'm not, but I'll wait in the car if it'll make you feel any better."

Villand squinted him up and down. "Okay. You can stay. So, what's this about?"

The interior of the house reflected the outside: complete and total neglect.

"Take a pew." Villand waved around the squalid living room. The carpet, once orange shag, was flattened to an evil reddish color with dark splotches interspersed with bald spots. Lev looked for somewhere to sit that wouldn't contaminate him and noticed Mel doing the same.

"Hey, don't stand on ceremony, sit anywhere."

Lev eased into a green leatherette easy chair with a Gaffer's tape patch on one arm; he didn't lean back. Mel perched on the edge of a wooden chair facing the TV while Villand dropped into a beanbag that barely changed shape under his skinny frame.

"I came to ask a couple of questions about Kate Keenan. She talked to you and Don Ames at the wrap party. I'm trying to locate Kate."

Villand's beady eyes darted to Mel. "So why's he here then?"

"He wants to find Kate, too."

"We weren't the only ones who spoke to her."

"I know. I want to speak with as many people as I can who saw her at the party."

"Yeah, okay. The last I saw her was when we were all told to leave by security. We said goodnight, then Don and me left. Kate was remained inside the building."

"What were you talking about?"

"Computers. Don was thinking of getting a new one and asked Kate what she was using."

"Unusual question to ask someone on the spur of the moment, wasn't it?"

"Dunno, it was just conversation."

"I was told that you and Don had been overheard agreeing you hoped something would happen to stop Primo's next film from being made."

"That's a lie."

"Wasn't Ames pissed-off that Kate was being considered to write Primo's film and not him?"

"Give me a break. You're an agent. It happens all the time. Writers and actors—bitch, bitch, bitch."

"Look, the chance of finding her is lessening by the

hour."

"The only people I recall talking to her other than Vicky, Stella and Chaz, were earlier in the evening before Primo came on stage."

"Who were they?"

"One was Hank Tolomeo. He was arguing." Villand lit a cigarette and blew a smoke beam toward the nicotine-stained ceiling.

"Arguing with whom?"

"Jilly Suede, that's all I know."

Jilly was Primo's assistant, Gal Friday and personal confidant. She'd been with Primo for more than twenty years.

Lev rose and walked to the door, Mel following like a pet dog. "Thanks for your time."

Villand remained sprawled on his beanbag. "If you hear of anyone in the business who could use my talents, Leventhal, let me know, okay?"

"Sure. I'll keep my ears open." All three knew Lev was lying.

"He wasn't much help," Mel said as they walked back to the car.

"Hank Tolomeo is one of the people on my list. I'll arrange a meeting with him."

"I know him. When would you like to talk to Hank?"

"Wait! You know Tolomeo?"

"He offered me a job with him when I was still at UCLA."

"And you went to Apple. Bet that didn't go over well."

"He's not that way. He does a lot of business with my father in India."

In the car, heading for the freeway, Lev asked, "What kind of business does your father do with TolomeoTechnics?"

"Dad runs a film studio in Mumbai." Mel smiled thinly. "I think you already knew that. Anyway, to answer your question, my Dad buys digital equipment from Hank."

Lev grunted. "From what I understand there are a few tricks we can learn from India in the area of digital film making."

"Yes, progress is very important to India. TolomeoTechnics advancements in fiber optics, computers and robotics have been amazing the last few years."

They were almost back at the office and Lev wanted to turn the conversation back to Tolomeo. "So when do you think you can get hold of him?"

"I'll call him tonight."

"That would be great."

Lev turned into his parking space behind his office; there were only three cars in the lot. "Which one are you, Mel?"

"Silver Audi," Mel pointed. "There, on the right."

Lev waited as Mel got in, turned on the motor, switched

on the headlights, gave a honk and drove out of the lot. Mel turned right on La Cienega.

Lev headed for the back door. He decided to check any messages or notes Joanie might have left for him. He stopped abruptly in the hallway when he heard the cough of a car engine starting. Easing the outside door open a few inches, he was able to make out the silhouette of a car with no lights move out of the driveway and turn in the same direction as Mel.

A. G. Hayes

Chapter 12

"You said this was going to be easy." Villand, hunched on his beanbag chair, had assumed a different one of his thousand faces: a scared-shitless face, a cigarette quivering between his lips, his phone pressed to his ear. "Leventhal was here with some young kid asking questions. Yeah, I let him in. What was I supposed to do?" Villand paused to listen to person on the other end of the phone, then added, "I don't know who the kid was, but he had an accent. Sounded like he was from India. Hindu, maybe." Stubbing out the cigarette, he shook another from a crumpled pack. "Listen, Ames, I don't like this." He tuned in to Ames and listened impatiently for awhile, finally interrupting: "No, I'll come over there. My place might be under surveillance."

A. G. Hayes

Chapter 13

Kate, dozing in her new office chair was startled by the sound of a key grating in the lock. *Scumbag must be back*, she told herself, and spun around to get a direct view of the metal door. It swung only partly open. Kate watched a cloth-covered tray being pushed across the threshold. The door then closed and she heard the lock reengage. Scumbag hadn't even entered.

Kate walked over to the tray, picked it up, and carried it back to her desk, where she removed the cloth. A hamburger and fries. She touched the bun with the back of her hand. Cold. The coffee however was lukewarm, and she noticed three chocolate chip cookies on top of an envelope. Taking a bite of one, she ripped open the envelope and removed a typewritten message: "Leave the computer on at all times."

Taking a second bite, she booted her computer. The "Welcome" button that was there earlier was gone. "Notes" and "Menu" were still there. "Notes" was glowing. Clicking on it, another message appeared: "Get some sleep. Tomorrow will be a busy day."

Having noticed that her built-in camera light was glowing slightly, she assumed that when she was anywhere in front of her computer she was also on closed circuit TV, she gave the camera lens the finger, picked up the coffee and the last two cookies, and headed for her cot.

Chapter 14

Lev dashed to his car, departed the parking lot, and hung a right. Both cars had turned north on La Cienega, heading towards Hollywood. He didn't know Mel's address but kept driving in the hope of catching up with the man's silver Audi. Then Lev called Joanie on his cellular.

"Joanie, it's me. Did you get an address for Mel Pashagora?

"No, why?"

Lev groaned, "Because you are always so efficient."

"Thanks. I did get his phone number."

"Give it to me, Joanie. It's very important."

"You expect me to remember it of the top of my head? It's nighttime and I'm at home! His numbers are in the daily log on my desk."

Lev pulled over. "Numbers?"

"He left both his home and cell. Where are you?"

"I'm in my car completing a U-turn in the middle of La Cienega." Lev sped back to the office and went straight to Joanie's desk, snapped on the lights and opened the log. Half way down the page, he saw Melhi Pashagora, with two phone numbers precisely written next to his name. Lev tapped in the cell number and waited. Four rings. Five. Something was wrong. He hit redial and heard, "Mel here." A wave of relief swept over him.

"Where are you, Mel?"

"I'm on my way home."

"What's your location?"

"Heading west on Sunset," replied Mel.

"How far from home?"

"Couple of miles. I live on Shoreham Drive."

"Anyone following you?"

"Following me? No."

"Keep an eye on the rearview mirror. What number on Shoreham?"

"Eighty-seven fifty. It's a condo. I'm in unit twelve-oh-eight."

Lev recalled the place: a high-rise overlooking the Strip. Exclusive digs with underground parking.

"Mel, listen to me. You know Vendome Liquor on Sunset?"

"Sure."

"Go in and wait until I get there. Tell the clerk you're being followed and you've called a buddy for backup. Okay?"

"What if he wants to call the police?"

"Fine. Let him. I'm on my way."

Lev screeched to a halt outside of Vendome Liquor, and

saw Mel standing inside at the counter talking to the clerk.

Mel turned nervously when Lev entered. "Ah, Lev. Bill here." He pointed to the man behind the counter. "He called the cops, but they said it wasn't enough to order a car directly there. Instead, they ordered a drive-by whenever a nearby cop car has the chance."

"Have they?"

"Not yet. Or if they did, they didn't stop," Mel said.

Lev glanced out the window as a customer pulled up. "Okay. I'll follow you up to your place." Turning to the clerk, Lev said, "Thanks pal."

"No problem, man."

They each drove up Shoreham into the underground parking lot, and then rode the elevator together to the twelfth floor.

A hundred feet west of Vendome Liquors, the man in a car parked on Sunset watched the arrival of Lev, then the departure of Mel's car followed by Lev's. He tagged along at a distance until they turned into an underground parking facility. The car did a U-turn and travelled back down to Sunset.

Mel's apartment was large and tastefully furnished.

"I could use a drink, how about you?" Mel asked.

"Small brandy would be fine, if you have it."

Mel removed his jacket and tossed it across the back of a ten-foot leather couch. "Coming up." He walked to a well-stocked drinks trolley while Lev stood in front of the floor-to-ceiling window and looked out across the twinkling lights of Hollywood below.

"Nice view, Mel."

"Everyone says that." Mel handed Lev a crystal snifter of brandy. Sipping his own drink, Mel asked, "So a car followed me out of your office parking lot?"

"Yeah," Lev said, swirling his brandy. "Whoever it was had evidently been waiting. When you left my place, he followed you, lights off. By the time I ran outside, the car was out of the driveway, and, dark like that, I couldn't see the license or make. Any idea who might want to follow you?"

"No."

Lev sipped his brandy. The disappearance of Kate, and the mysterious tail on Mel made him wonder about their connection. At this rate, the next to vanish could be Mel.

"Okay. Keep your door locked and bolted, and get a good night's sleep. Call your office tomorrow and say you need a couple of days off. I'll pick you up around nine. We'll work together, checking any further leads."

"I do have personal time due," Mel commented.

"Fine, then that's settled."

"Wait, Lev. Before you go I want to call Tolomeo. I know it's late, but I'd like to make an appointment for us to see him first thing tomorrow."

Lev grinned, toasted Mel, then sank into a comfortable armchair while Mel made the call. Hank Tolomeo answered on the first ring.

"Hank, this is Mel. Hope I'm not calling too late." He glanced at Lev. "Good. Listen, I have a favor to ask. Someone would like to talk to you before you head back to Palo Alto tomorrow. Won't take long. It's about my friend, Kate. I believe you met her once." Mel shook his head in the negative and laughed. "No, Hank, he's her agent." Shaking his head in the positive and smiling at Lev, he continued, "Thanks. See you at ten," and hung up. "Hank wanted to know if you were a cop. He's heading north later in the morning but can see us at ten at his office."

"Perfect. Then you and I will meet as planned at nine and we'll go in my car."

As Lev drove down the hill and turned west on Sunset, he took a deep breath. His mind was running in too many directions.

He toyed with the thought of driving north along the coastal highway to Malibu. The sea air would clear his head and allow him think better; however, a couple of miles down Sunset, amidst the glow of neon signs, he saw a sign that made him change his mind. It was the big red and yellow marquee of Charlie V's. The building stood on the site of the old Ciro's, a celebrity nightclub of the thirties and forties that faded in the late 1950s and eventually disappeared.

He drove into the parking lot and switched off the engine. A parking attendant immediately opened the car door.

Inside the nightclub, a quartet on stage was blasting out a tune Lev had heard before, but couldn't name. A dozen couples were together on a diminutive dance floor. He was ushered to a small table, and while a waiter in black tux awaited his order, a voice he recognized at once wafted from over his left shoulder. The voice was that of Pattie Primo.

"Lev! I haven't seen you in ages, darling. How are you?"

There she was, Primo's grieving widow, dressed in a black low cut evening gown with several thousand dollars-worth of diamonds draped around her neck.

Lev signalled the waiter away, stood, turned and took her hand. "Pattie. I'm so sorry about Frank. It was all so sudden."

"Yes, it was. You will be at the service tomorrow, won't you?"

"Of course I will. He'll be missed. The town won't be the same without him." He had no idea when or where the service was going to be.

"Thank you, Lev. So glad I bumped into you. I'll look for you tomorrow at the service." She turned and swirled away into the darkness.

It was then he decided to see if Charles Vance was in the club. Signaling to the the waiter he'd just dismissed, he asked if the owner was in the club tonight.

Realizing Lev was not going to order, the surly waiter replied, "I'll try to locate him for you."

Lev left the table and sat at the bar sipping soda water for ten long minutes. When the waiter didn't return, he decided to leave and call Charles. As Lev headed for the door, he noticed one of the bartenders who had been eyeing him pull out a cell phone, turn away and begin talking.

He was standing outside with some other patrons waiting for their cars, when he checked his wristwatch. It was after midnight, so he decided the trip to Malibu was out. He had a lot to complete the next day and if he didn't get a lead on Kate soon, she'd officially become a missing person and a police matter.

A. G. Hayes

Chapter 15

Kate slept a fitful couple hours before being jolting awake. There was someone in the vault! She moved her head to hear more clearly, but all was silent. She was certain she'd heard something in the main room. Her heart pounded and she broke into a cold sweat. The door to her "bedroom" was closed but it didn't have a lock—anyone could walk right in.

Easing off the cot, she crept barefoot toward the door, arms outstretched, praying not to trip over anything. The coldness of the concrete floor instantly began creeping into her legs. At the door, she remained motionless, straining to hear the slightest sound. She had no means of defense. Should she open the door and go further, or remain in the cell and wait until whoever it was burst in and overwhelmed her? Making up her mind, she eased the door open a few inches, peered into the main room and saw her computer on the desk, it's screen still brightly lit. There was that sound again! Something or someone was out there. She quickly pulled the door shut.

Now fully awake, she realized she'd heard that kind of thrumming, whirring, jingly sound before. Then she remembered. Robotics! She'd participated in various robot classes at

UCLA and had become fascinated with the possibilities for their future use in the making of movies. There was a robot at loose inside the vault!

She tweaked the door open and this time gasped aloud. Standing sentinel-like outside her door was a squat, four-foot-tall Robo-Cop-like piece of complicated electronic equipment. The robot, claw-like pincers hanging at it's side, continued whirring lowly but remained completely motionless.

Pushing the door wider, Kate walked into the room and turned to face it. The previously inert-appearing robot immediately spun its head in her direction, revealing a compact video camera where it's head should have been. A synthesized voice rasped, "I'm sorry. I did not mean to wake you, Kate. Please forgive me."

"Who are you?" Kate hoped her voice didn't reveal her fear.

"Your constant companion and intermediary, when your human guardian isn't here, until you have completed your assignment."

"I was told to communicate through my computer."

"That is correct. I am here as extra precaution against unforeseen problems."

"Meaning what?"

The damn thing ignored her question, offering instead, "There is a change of clothes for you on the bench over there.

I thought they might make you feel more comfortable."

No words were exchanged while she crossed to the bench where found a carryon sized soft bag. The robot's video eye, however, followed her to the bench and as she returned to her bedroom cell.

Kate closed the door and checked out the bag. Everything provided fit her perfectly: clean jeans, a turtleneck sweater and a pair of Nikes. Whoever had captured her knew her exact sizes. After changing, Kate headed back to the main room, the robot's video eye following her.

"I am programmed to recognize your presence whenever you are within fifty feet of me."

Kate sat at the desk, selected "Notes," and typed on her computer, "Who the hell is this robot?"

The reply was instantaneous: "You are a light sleeper, Kate. Rob doesn't usually awaken people."

"He did me," she tapped. "So I'm a prisoner in a film vault with a robot jailer. Unless I'm released immediately I'll press charges for holding me against my will."

"Sorry to hear that, Kate," came the reply. "I'm not sure anyone has ever pressed charges like that against a robot. But more importantly, unless you do exactly as you are told, your friend Mel may never see his father in India again, and that would be a real pity."

Kate stared at the screen as more appeared.

"No more talk. You are safe as long as you follow orders. I've programmed Rob to be your constant guardian until the assignment is finished." Kate heard the robot Rob roll forward and stop next to her.

"Stay seated and turn toward me," Rob commanded.

Kate angrily spun her chair until they were eye-to-eye.

"Place the palm of your right hand on the flat pad next to the video camera and stare into the lens."

She did as ordered, and three seconds later the robot said, "Your hand and fingerprints, iris and retinal patterns, heart rate, blood pressure and other pertinent identifying data are now successfully recorded in my memory. As long as I am near you, no harm can come to you."

She growled, "Protected! Prisoner is more like it."

Rob simply turned and rolled back to his post in front of the door to her makeshift bedroom.

Chapter 16

Franz Villand's '96 Chevy was half way down Vineland Avenue when his cell chirped. Driving with one hand, he searched his pockets. "Sonofabitch." The chirping continued and Villand finally clawed the phone from an inside pocket.

"Yeah, who is this? I can hardly hear you. Talk louder." Villand hated cells; he was always either losing or having trouble hearing them. He was, nonetheless, carrying one in the hope that his agent might contact him in a hurry with a job. Fat chance. "I said I was coming over to your place. What do you mean, telling me now that you don't want me to? Why not?" Villand paused to receive Ames reply. "I might be followed and you don't want to be implicated? Ames, are you crazy? *You* involved *me!*" Villand stopped for a red light and the engine quit. "Shit! No, I stopped at a light and the car quit. Something about the carburetor. Gotta' get it fixed." Villand cranked the engine, listening to each groaning revolution get slower and weaker, praying the battery would hold up. The engine finally caught and he moved the car forward. "So where you wanna' meet? Okay. Yeah, yeah, I'll keep checking I'm not being tailed."

A. G. Hayes

Chapter 17

Mel was waiting outside the entrance to the underground garage of Shoreham Towers when Lev drove up the hill, pulled to the curb, leaned over, and opened the passenger side door.

"Morning, Lev." Mel folded into the seat and snapped on the seat belt.

"Sleep well?" Lev asked as he pulled away.

"Better than I thought I would."

"Good. Where do we meet Hank Tolomeo?"

"Marina Del Rey."

"I thought he lived in Palo Alto."

"His plant is in Palo Alto. When he's in Southern California he lives on his boat and does most of his business by video conference from his office in the Marina."

"What kind of man am I going to meet, Mel?" Lev honked the horn as a messenger on a ten-speed, cut between his radiator and the trunk of a Mercedes.

"Hank's a nice guy when you get to know him."

"How long does that take?"

"Depends," muttered Mel.

Lev nodded, "On what?"

"Well, you know." Mel tipped one hand side to side. "He's usually at his best in the mornings. You'll get along fine with him. You seem like a people-person type of guy."

"In my business I have to be."

Mel leaned back, and explained that he'd met Hank while attending classes at UCLA. The moment they met, they struck up a friendship of sorts. He'd have dinner with Hank every few months or so, and they'd talk about Mel's father, Indian movies, and how Hank hoped his dad would travel someday to LA. Hank said he wanted to show the man around his plant. Mel's dad, however, didn't like flying. It made his feet swell, even in first class, Mel's father complained.

"So Hank and your father do business together?"

"To quote Hank," Mel said, "'top secret genius stuff.'"

Lev made the transition onto the San Diego Freeway. "Sounds like the kind of guy who doesn't play poker with his back to a mirror."

Mel chuckled. "He doesn't."

The traffic was now up to its usual 75 miles per hour, and traffic was nose to tail despite the speed. Lev completed the transition to the Marina Freeway and approached Lincoln Boulevard, where Mel began giving directions.

"Once on Lincoln, stay in the right lane. The office is about a mile on our left. A three story beige colored building just beyond a small boat yard, you'll see it."

A few minutes later, Lev saw the building and asked about parking. "Around the back, turn into the driveway. That's Hank's car." Mel pointed to a silver 1938 SS Jaguar sitting close to the back entrance.

"A car buff, too," Lev grunted as he pulled into the first available slot.

"Hank has many expensive things, Lev."

The door to Hank's outer office swung open before Mel could turn the knob.

"Hi, come on in." A smiling young woman held the door open. "He's waiting for you, Mr. Pashagora."

"Thanks, Sue." Mel turned to Lev. "This is Sue Hawkins, Hank's Southern California Rep. Sue, meet Lev Leventhal."

Lev trailed Mel into an inner office. Mel knocked once at the door and entered.

A heavyset man sat behind a refectory table he used as a desk. Piles of books and papers were scattered across the mahogany surface.

"Mel! Come on in! Sit down!" He pushed out of his throne-like chair, waddled around the table and gave Mel a hug and a brisk slap on the back. Hank Tolomeo was an inch shorter than Mel and at least seventy pounds heavier. His dark hair showed flashes of gray at the temples. He wore a pair of Maui Jim sunglasses pushed up on his forehead. Hank scrutinized Lev with his inquiring kelly green eyes. "Glad you called, Mel, it's been too long since I've seen you."

Mel grinned, "Just over a month, Hank."

"Too long. Now sit down, both of you." He waved in the direction of two slate-gray leather armchairs facing the table. "You must be Lev Leventhal, Kate's agent." He offered a beefy hand. A single strong squeeze and he returned to his throne. "So bring me up to date about Kate."

Hank remained silent as Mel and Lev went through their last couple of days searching for Kate.

"You'd like to know when I last saw her, right?"

Mel nodded.

"Primo and I were having a drink before he went on stage. He'd told me he was going to make an innovative movie with a young woman with a big future. He was very excited. Said it would be a closed set production. Already there were rumors surrounding the secrecy. Primo was no fool. He knew the power of gossip in Hollywood. Primo pointed Kate out to me. She was talking to Stella Rae and the actor, what's his name?"

"Chaz Falconer," said Lev.

"Whatever. That was the last time I saw her."

Lev leaned forward. "Frank Primo was hyping his new movie to you just before he went on stage?"

"Yes, he was."

"It was common knowledge in town that you, Primo, and Jilly Suede, not Kate, would be working closely together with him on the production."

Hank's green eyes flashed. "How do you mean?"

"Rumor has it that TolomeoTechnics was going to 'revolutionize the movie industry'."

"Who told you that?"

"Stacy Hart."

"See? Primo knew the right places to drop hints. Well, it's obvious the film won't be made and TT won't be involved, so it's of little consequence. I'll admit my company is working on a system to bring movie making into the twenty-first century." He nodded to Mel. "My company has been working closely with his father's for some time."

Given what he was hearing, Lev decided not to reveal that he understood some of Kate's own revolutionary technology. It was better, he decided, that Hank feel he was in complete control. That way, he might reveal an additional kernel or two of information.

"So no one you've questioned saw Kate after the party, right?" Tolomeo asked.

Lev nodded. "Correct."

"You said when you went to her house her computer was missing and the place had been tossed. What feedback did you get from the cops?"

Lev paused a moment. "Burglary, no prints. No different from a couple a hundred others that happen in LA each day."

Hank switched to Mel. "Any idea what was on the computer that would make it important enough to steal? I mean like anything she would rather not have anyone besides herself see?"

Mel shrugged. "Maybe a treatment of the script she was doing for Primo."

"Primo, would have had a copy, of course."

Lev cut in. "No. She pitched to Primo over the phone and he's agreed to meet her after the party. They'd never met in person. Kate was going to give Primo a demo of her work on her laptop after the wrap party." Lev omitted mention of the device she'd entrusted to him.

Hank frowned. "No else one at the studio was involved in the decision?"

"You know Primo," Lev offered. "He owned the studio, always did whatever he wanted. He often made deals in secret one-on-one. Everyone in town knew that."

"Yes, of course," Hank snorted. "It's still a curious way to do business in this day and age."

"Absolutely, I agree," Mel said. "However, Primo was always different."

"So Kate and her laptop are both missing, and who ever has her, also has a copy of her work, if nothing else from inside her mind."

"Whether they had Kate or the computer or both, they'd still have to open and run the program to see what she'd written," Mel added.

"Shouldn't be a problem. There are plenty of hackers around."

"True. However, I know Kate. Anyone attempting to hack her computer would find nothing if they did succeed. All they'd get would be a pile of sizzling metal and plastic."

Hank's eyebrows arched. "Self-destruct! Then Kate would have no back up."

"Kate backed up everything she wrote. Copied it to a second computer for safety. Every word, every night, she transferred the latest version without fail," Mel said.

"Where is this second computer?" Hank asked.

"Can't help you there. But Kate said her work was completely safe once she made the transfer."

Hank looked dubious. "Weren't you curious? You're her best friend."

"A secret remains a secret only when it's known to but one person."

Hank glanced at his watch. "Well, I have to go, Mel. Hope it wasn't a waste your time, Lev."

"Actually, you've been a big help," Lev replied. "We appreciate your time."

Mel stood. "I'll tell my father we saw each other when I call him this weekend."

"You do that, and let's get together for lunch soon."

Chapter 18

Back in the car, Lev phoned Joanie and instructed her to contact Jilly Suede. He needed personnel and parking permits for entry onto the Megastar movie lot, for a "drive-on" for Mel and himself; they'd be at the studio gate in forty minutes to pick them up. Ten minutes later, Joanie called back. "Okay, the passes will be at the gate. Don't forget: Primo's memorial is at three this afternoon at the Wee Kirk 'O the Heather in Forest Lawn-Glendale. Stacy phoned and said to tell you to get there early. She has something for you." Joanie paused. "You didn't mention anything about a service, Lev."

"I only found out last night. Sorry."

"Thanks, Lev." She replied testily and hung up.

Lev asked Mel, "Does Kate have any ex-boyfriends, anyone who might have a grudge against her?"

"Not that I know of. There was a guy who said he was a Hollywood writer. He'd somehow gotten hold of Kate's phone number and he kept calling her at home."

"Do you know his name?"

"Don Ames. I heard Villand mention the name when we were at Villand's last night.

"What did he want?"

"He'd found out she was a screenwriter and student at UCLA, and wanted to meet her, saying he could maybe help her find a producer for her scripts. We both knew that was bullshit, as Ames hadn't sold anything in years."

"How'd you find that out?"

"Easy. I called a couple of friends. One of them advised me Ames had tried to sue a major studio a while back claiming they'd stolen one of his stories. He's never worked since. From what I can tell, no one would ever want to steal any of his work."

"Did Ames ever try to contact you?"

"No."

Lev thought that odd. If Ames knew Kate had been studying at the UCLA, he must have done some research, and Mel's name would certainly have come up somewhere along the line.

Mel shifted uneasily in his seat. "After we've visited the studio, could you drop me off at Shoreham? Memorials depress me."

"Do you want to go home now? I can drop you off. Sunset Boulevard is coming up ahead."

"That's okay, Megastar movie lot first. I want to help all I can."

The guard handed the passes through the gatehouse window. "Leave them in view on the dash while you're on the lot.

Drop them off when you leave, Mr. Leventhal."

Driving onto the lot, they headed toward the Megastar building located midway between the main gate and the first sound stage.

"Where was the wrap party held, Lev?"

"Stage four. Why?"

"Just wondered. Kate invited me to go with her. Said she wanted me to meet her new agent."

"I wish you'd taken her up on it," Lev said. A group of extras dressed as cowboys sauntered past, and a forklift loaded with fake Alpine landscaping rumbled in the opposite direction.

"I can't help thinking that if I'd been there, this might have never happened," Mel said.

"I didn't mean it that way, Mel."

"I know, but that's how I feel. I have ever since I heard she'd gone missing," Mel explained.

Lev pulled into an empty visitor's slot. The time was eleven fifteen. "Let's go meet Jilly Suede. Jilly's been Primo's personal assistant for over twenty years. She knows everything that goes on at Megastar. Maybe we can get her to join us for an early lunch in the commissary."

Lev had gotten to know Jilly over the years when he'd accompanied his writers to Megastar for various story meetings. Somehow, she always managed to spend at least a few minutes with him at every meeting. Jilly was somewhere in her early forties, single, and all business. When they arrived at her office and he asked to see her, they were told she had taken a couple of days hiatus.

"My secretary just phoned Jilly and got us a couple of passes," Lev said. The receptionist smiled. "Yes, I know. I know who you are, so I called the gate."

"Will Jilly be at the memorial this afternoon?" Lev asked.

"Yes, well, at least I suppose so. I phoned her home and left a message on her machine. The memorial date change was a sudden decision by Mrs. Primo. Originally it was to be next week."

Lev asked, "Any idea why it was fast forwarded?"

"No. We received the memo late yesterday afternoon."

Lev thanked her. Mel suggested they take a walk and check out stage four.

It was not to be.

A red light flashing outside the entrance to the building, indicated that shooting was in progress. While they waited for the green light, Lev checked around the area. There was the usual clutter of scenery and portable arc lamps parked in the street with electric golf carts and trucks flowing past, a typical studio day.

"Did everyone leave the party through this door?" Mel asked.

"As far as I recall, security ordered people to leave and directed them to this door. I don't recall them directing guests to any other exits."

"Then Kate most likely left the party here." Mel sounded as if he were assuring himself that Kate was not still somewhere in the huge building. Lev glanced back toward the main gate, up the street toward the back lot, with Mount Lee rising behind the studio.

"You think she might still be on the lot?" Lev asked.

Mel didn't answer, but he walked slowly along the side of the sound stage pointing toward the back lot, then quickly bent down and scooped something off the ground. He cupped it in his palm as he turned and walked back to Lev.

"This is one of Kate's earrings. It's one of a pair I gave her for her birthday last year. That means that Kate was here, and wherever Kate is, she didn't go willingly."

A. G. Hayes

Chapter 19

Kate was half-asleep in her chair when the "Notes" button on her computer screen began flashing. The robot was on sentry duty, silent as a moorland hillside.

Clicking on the button, a message appeared stating simply: "This is today's assignment: I want you to write the first act of the screenplay you pitched to Primo."

Kate stared at the words, and then typed. "I need a hot shower first."

"First, carry out today's assignment," came the response.

"I need a hot shower, clean underwear and sanitary living conditions."

"You are a prisoner. Obey orders."

Already the musky odor of her body was beginning to mix with the staleness of the air, despite the year round air conditioning mentioned by 'Scumbag' on her arrival. "I don't have my notes. They're in my home office."

"Check the top right hand drawer of the desk. You will find everything you need there."

Two clicks sounded from the drawer that she'd attempted without success to open earlier. It slid open with ease. There were her outline notes, and a spiral notebook along with the yellow legal pad she used in her home office.

The assignment is to write the first act, but for whom am I writing it? she wondered. She glanced at the screen. It was blank. *At least whoever it is isn't telepathic.*

This is ridiculous, her mind screamed, *bossed around by a computer screen and monitored by a robot. Whoever's holding me thinks Primo was interested in a screenplay. that means that just perhaps, he or she doesn't know about my program!*

Rob whirred and rolled his way over to the desk and rasped, "Begin work, Kate. Begin now."

Chapter 20

Lev stopped the car next to the main gate security office, scooped the passes off the dash and headed inside. Mel remained in the car staring at the diamond earring in his hand.

"You can't park there, Mr. Leventhal." Luckily, it was one of the guards he'd known for years.

"I know, but I need to ask you a quick question, Mike." Lev handed him the passes. "The other night, when Mr. Primo died on stage four, did all the guests return their passes?"

"I assume so. Studio rules, you know, and with security being increased nationwide, I'm pretty certain they all were."

"You know someone went missing that night, yes?"

"I was informed today when the police came asking questions—it was a writer, a young woman."

"She's a client of mine, and we drove on the lot together. After Mr. Primo died, there was a lot of confusion and I couldn't locate her. I searched until the crowds had thinned, and security demanded everyone leave. I concluded she'd met some friends and left with them. When I drove off the lot with all the others, the guard simply waved me through without asking for my pass. I didn't think about it at the time, I was still concerned as to her whereabouts. The passes were still on the dash of my car the next morning."

Mike looked embarrassed. "Given the uproar, it is possible some of the passes weren't collected."

"So my missing client could have just as easily been driven off the lot by someone without showing a pass."

"I'm afraid so, Mr. Leventhal."

"Thanks, Mike. If you hear anything, let me know." He placed one of his business cards on the security guard's desk.

"Sure will, and I'm sorry about the break down in procedure."

Returning to the car, Lev brought Mel up to date.

"If that's the case, Kate's abductor could have been anyone on the lot, not just guests on the A list."

Mel opened his hand and gently bounced the diamond. "And she could equally still be somewhere on the lot."

With those chilling thoughts in mind, Lev headed back into Hollywood to drop Mel off at Shoreham before going to the memorial service. He intended to arrive early enough to have plenty of time to talk with Stacy Hart.

The massive wrought-iron gates of Forrest Lawn-Glendale were wide open, making Lev think of the Pearly Gates of Heaven, although he felt sure that many of the departed who went through the iron gates feet first would never make it through the Pearly ones. Hollywood celebrities used

Forrest Lawn for weddings and funerals, the funerals being by far the more lasting of the two.

Over the years, he'd been to several final farewells, and was familiar with the location of the beautiful little church, The Wee Kirk O' the Heather. When he arrived, he noticed a solitary car in the parking lot, and recognized it at once as Stacy Hart's.

On closer examination, the car was locked and she was nowhere in sight. He looked inside the church; empty except for a woman arranging flowers on the altar. Checking the time, he saw it was a little before two, and decided to walk around the outside of the church and think. He'd almost made a complete circuit when he saw Stace sitting on a bench beneath a willow tree, writing in a notebook. She glanced up and waved as he approached. "I didn't expect you quite this early, Lev."

"Joanie told me you had something for me." As he sat next to her, she closed her notebook.

"I do. I discovered Charles Vance was heavily in debt to Primo. In fact, he was close to losing his club."

"Oh, boy," Lev muttered.

"That's why I called. It seems the debt had grown over the last year, with Primo lending good money after bad. There were no actual legal papers signed. It was purely personal friend-to-friend hand written IOU's from Vance to Primo.

Well, the last couple of months, the debt grew beyond a handshake and Primo pressed Vance for a conclusion, either in cash or through forfeiture of the club."

"How did you find out?"

"Jilly Suede," Stace said softly.

"She who knows all when it comes to Frank Primo's personal and business life, right?"

"Yes," Stacy agreed.

"How much are we talking about?" Lev asked.

"A million five."

Lev gazed across the green manicured lawns, curving amid trees and gardens, that peacefully containing the souls of those who now had no such problems. "Where does Jilly come in?"

"She notarized the IOU's. Primo, like many executives relied on Jilly to take care of details, even personal ones. Jilly also mentioned that Primo had assured her that she would be remembered in his Will, and would be safe and comfortable after he'd gone."

"Perhaps she feels Primo should receive his loan in full and wants to be sure the million five is paid back."

Stacy sighed, "No doubt. Only natural, I suppose."

They watched in silence as a couple of limos slowly drove up the hill toward the church, no doubt the vanguard of many.

"Did you know Jilly's taken a couple of days off?" Lev asked.

Stace looked toward the church where the cars were parking. "Yes, she phoned me a couple of hours before I left to come here."

"Will she be at the service?"

"Of course she will."

A few more early arrivals were making their way up the hill, and groups of people in the parking lot were chatting with that air of uncomfortable tension that often accompanies such affairs. A couple of young men in dark suits stood in the church vestibule handing out programs to those entering. Lev checked the time. "It's twenty to three."

Stace nodded at the road winding up from the main gates. "It's going to be a big send off for Primo," she said sadly. The line of vehicles had now increased to a slow crawling procession inching up the hill.

They rose from the bench and sauntered toward the church. As they drew closer, they could hear the sound of the church organ playing a medley of tunes from past Broadway hit musicals. At least the theme of the memorial would be what Primo loved best: show business. Stace raised her eyebrows and smiled as they entered the church.

They sat in a row near the back, which give them an excellent position to observe the mourners arrive and take their seats. Lev noticed Vicky Vance and Pattie Primo already seated in the first row along with Stella Rae, Chaz Falconer and Jilly Suede.

The music played quietly on, blending with the hushed murmurs of the congregation, until piped-in music began playing through the faux organ pipes in the choir loft.

The last of the invited had finally taken their seats and the music faded, as the minister, in surplice, walked to the altar and faced the beloved. Pink-faced and white-haired, he looked the perfect clergyman as he laid his heavy leather bound prayer book on the lectern.

He began to eulogize the life and virtues of Francis Primo, his deep droning tones continuing for almost ten minutes. Finally he ended with, "And so, as we are gathered here today to remember Francis, if there are those among us who wish to say a few final words, please step forward."

Lev watched as men and women from the congregation went one-by-one to the lectern to speak. Some of the epitaphs were amusing, others simply said how much he'd be missed. The last speaker had returned to his seat when the organ softly crescendoed to a heart-pulling rendition of "Going Home." Then from the choir loft, a beautiful tenor voice sailed out. People, surprised, turned to see Charles Vance standing alone at the choir rail, singing,

I'm going home, I'm going home

When my life here is o'er, I'm going home

Won't it be so sweet, to rest at Jesus' feet

When my life here is o'er, I'm going home

I'm traveling in the light

And my way is clear and bright

Some glad day I'm going home

Heading for the pearly gates for there my

Savior waits when my life here is o'er, I'm going home.

When the last lyrics soared out across the church and the music faded, there was absolute silence from the congregation. Then a burst of applause quickly grew and filled the place of worship. Everyone present knew Primo would have approved. It had been years since Lev had heard Charles sing and he'd never sounded better.

"That was beautiful," Stacy said quietly. "What a breathtaking end."

People filing out glanced up at the choir loft, but Vance was no longer in sight. Outside, the usual quiet conversations began bubbling up, most surrounding Vance's solo.

"I had no idea Charles was going to sing, I think it was wonderful. Primo would have loved it. They were such good friends, you know."

Stace and Lev glanced at Vicky Vance, making her gushing remarks to the clergyman.

"It was a last minute decision," the minister replied. "Mr. Vance brought a tape recording of the organ music and we just slipped it in at the end."

"I must find Charles and thank him," Pattie Primo simpered to Vicky Vance. "Where is that wonderful man?"

Many of the cars had already left, going toward the reception at Musso and Franks on Hollywood Boulevard. Lev told Stace he would see her at the reception, and was heading to his car when he heard two horrifying screams. Vicky Vance and Pattie Primo were rushing wildly from the church, their faces ashen, eyes wide with horror. Lev raced toward them and was among the first to arrive at their side. Vicky Vance collapsed in his arms. "Charles is dead! He's been murdered!"

Pattie pointed a trembling finger at the church. "He's up in the choir loft, a knife in his back."

Lev's first reaction was that the murderer must still be in the church. He started for the entrance when he felt a hand grab his shoulder. Turning, he looked into the face of Hank Tolomeo holding a cell phone.

"What's happening?" Hank asked. "I was phoning for a cab when I heard the screams."

"I didn't know you were here, Hank."

"Almost wasn't. I was in a cab on my way to the airport

when I got a call on my cell, saying the memorial service had been moved up to today at three. I arrived just as Charles was ending his hymn."

"Charles is dead. Someone stabbed him."

Hank blanched. "Oh, my God!"

Someone brought a couple of chairs from the church, and deposited limp Vicky Vance into one. Pattie Primo plopped down on the other and sipped from a proffered glass of water. Cars stopped. Car doors opened. People spilled out on to the parking lot all talking at once.

"I'm going inside," Lev said.

"Right, I'll come with you," Hank said.

The minister, his voice quivering, stood shaking at the foot of the stairway to the choir loft.

"No one can go up, gentlemen. Police orders. I informed them at once, and was given strict instructions to allow no one into the loft. Our heavenly loft has become a crime scene."

As if on cue, police sirens appeared, quickly winding down and groaning into silence. Two black and whites slowed to a halt and parked at 90-degree angles outside the church blocking access. Seconds later, an unmarked Crown Vic squeezed around them.

Stace grasped Lev's arm. "I think we should leave while we can." As Lev turned to speak, he noticed Hank was gone.

A. G. Hayes

Chapter 21

Kate switched off the computer. No way was she going to type a draft, notes or not.

"You were told not to turn off the computer, Kate," Rob announced.

"Fuck you, Rob."

"You will be punished, Kate." Rob extended a long pincher arm and turned the computer back on.

Kate switched it off and pulled out both the wall plug and the yellow cable.

"Go ahead. Plug them back in, smart ass."

There was no way. Rob had no knees, and he couldn't bend at the waist. The video camera where his head should have been turned, and she heard the hum of the zoom motor as he zeroed in close.

"Kate. Mel will suffer. Plug in the computer and the cable. Hurry."

That was it! Her pent up resentment exploded, and she shoved back her chair, directing the high leather back into Rob's mid-section.

Rob didn't budge. "If you feel the need to communicate, then do it through me," Rob said. "Then write the outline. In the morning you will feel better and have a visitor."

"I have to go to the bathroom."

"No problem, Kate. You will be perfectly safe. I will stand guard and protect you," Rob replied, moving toward the meager washroom and stopping at the side of its doorless arch.

Kate followed into the decrepit washroom and, sitting on the closed toilet seat, began looking for anything she could use to put Rob out of action and escape. The air conditioning duct that ran the length of the main room caught her eye. Mid-room, an industrial-sized air vent dropped down and opened over one of the benches. *There's no air conditioner in the room, so it must be located outside the vault. Could I use that vent as a means of escape?* she asked herself. The answer was, in order to find out, she must first immobilize the tin man.

Flushing the toilet to cover her thought-pause, she returned to the main room and began searching.

A careful examination revealed an old paperback, a book of matches tucked inside the cellophane wrapper of a crumpled cigarette pack, an old can of spray paint and an old rag mop. Shaking the paint can, she pressed the button. A stream of black paint surged out. Her heart beating hard, she collected everything, reviewed her plan in her mind, took a deep breath and returned to the toilet. After a few moments, she called from inside, "I need your help here, Rob."

Clinking and whirring, Rob centered himself in the center of the archway. His synthesized voice rasped. "What is the problem, the plumbing?"

"It's your damn presence!" she yelled, holding the spray paint behind her back while making sure the mop was in a place she could easily reach.

The diminutive four-foot creep moved slightly forward, then stopped. "What is the problem, Kate?"

Stepping forward, Kate aimed the spray can at his video eye and pressed the plunger. A jet of black paint hit the lens and splattered down the front of his metallic chest. Kate grabbed the mop, stuffed the handle underneath him and twisted hard. He went over like a ninepin, hitting the floor flat on his back. In this position, he was as helpless as a turtle on its back. He couldn't see. He couldn't recover upright. His metallic voice screeched as he wildly flailed his pincer arms.

"You're mine now, you little bastard," Kate hissed, "and you can lay there until you blow a fuse." She removed the shaft of the mop and thrust it like a lance, plunging the end directly into Rob's electronic eye. With a hiss of air, the vision unit imploded.

A. G. Hayes

Chapter 22

Lev and Stace never made it out of the parking lot. Another Black and White blocked the backed the gate, its blaring speaker ordering everyone to leave his or her cars and re-enter the church.

"What about those who've left already?" Stace asked.

"The cops will undoubtedly visit them at home. Might as well get it over with now."

Back in the church, the mourners were shepherded to sit in the first few rows. Lev noticed more than half the original congregation had made it out of the parking lot before the discovery of Charles' demise.

Two men in dark suites stood facing them. The taller of the duo, a skinny guy with a dour face took over.

"I'm Agent Harcourt." He moved his gaze towards his shorter partner. "This is Agent Kirkland. We're FBI working with The Office of Homeland Security." Before anyone could question his authority, he explained, "Yes, this is a police crime scene. Nonetheless, we have questions for folks."

The questioning was polite and professional. Held at a small table set up at the side altar, Agent Harcourt asked the questions, and Agent Kirkland took notes. Harcourt began by asking if they had seen anyone leave the choir loft at the end of the service. Lev noticed the two Feds exchange tired glances as each occupant answered no to this and every other question of the rest of the half hour.

Finished, Lev and Stacy drove down the twisty road from the church and through the gate. They had agreed to meet at the Musso and Frank's, a celebrity restaurant in Hollywood after Lev picked up Mel.

"This wake would bring a smile to the lips of the Devil himself," the widow Primo said as she sipped champagne. Vicki was already writing her column in her head.

"You sure you feel up to this, Pattie?" Stella Rae muttered, scanning the crowded room.

"I feel better among friends." Pattie held out her empty glass to a passing waiter who swapped it for a full one. "Everyone who's anyone will end up here tonight. No one misses a free meal at Musso and Frank's."

"Any news on Kate?" Stella asked.

"Not yet." Pattie set her drink on a side table. "To tell you the truth, Stella, I know nothing about the girl and neither do the cops."

"Welcome to a Hollywood wake," Lev said as the two entered the standing room only restaurant. "Do they do things this way in India?"

Mel shook his head in the negative. "Not exactly." It was

his first glimpse of raw Hollywood self-indulgence. "Things are a little more subdued, except for the funeral pyre."

"Well put, Mel," Lev replied, grabbing two flutes of champagne and offering one to his friend.

A. G. Hayes

Chapter 23

Don Ames wished he'd never become involved. He'd once been a man about town, making loads of money. Nice clothes, several luxury cars, great apartment and plenty of women. Then four years ago, he began a downward spiral. He blamed his agent, bad mouthed the wrong people in the right places, and that was the end of his career as a writer. Sitting in a red plastic chair in the snack bar of the Hollywood K-Mart he looked in astonishment at the scrawny looking woman wearing too much mascara sitting opposite him.

"You went to Primo's memorial looking like that?"

Villand looked pained. "I'm a pro. No one recognized me."

Ames sucked the last of his Big Gulp. "I bet. It's a wonder the ushers let you in."

"I sat in the back row, slipped away and did what I was told, then returned to the back row without anyone noticing. I was first outta' there before the cops arrived."

"You're lucky your car started."

"Okay, so what's next? Or are we just going to keep meeting in places like this?"

Ames glanced around, "Until further orders."

"I don't know Ames, first Primo then Charles."

"And no more phone calls between us," Ames said. "See that phone on the wall?"

Villand nodded, "Yeah."

"You be next to it every day at ten o'clock in the morning starting tomorrow. She'll phone you."

"The K-Mart North Hollywood would be more convenient for me."

"Fine, *you* tell her that. I'm out of here. Wait five minutes, then you leave."

Villand snapped his purse open, removed a makeup mirror and checked his lipstick.

Chapter 24

Jilly Suede sat curled in the big swivel chair behind Primo's desk wondering how many times over the years she'd sat opposite him taking letters, notes, and attending to so many details of his business. She knew when his Will was read and the news came out that Primo had bequeathed her the studio and home, Pattie Primo would go ballistic and immediately contest the will. Especially the house. Pattie would try to uncover any lever that might keep her from losing the house and its contents to Jilly. It wouldn't work, though, as Primo's Will was clear. In the end, Pattie would end up with a token one dollar a year for the rest of her rotten, backbiting life. Jilly snuggled deeper into the chair. Two days from now, all this and more would be hers.

Tapping a French-manicured fingernail on top of the highly polished mahogany desk, Jilly smiled. She'd be very rich in a couple of days, a lot richer than most of the bitches she'd had to put up with over the years.

She would own Megastar studios due to Primo's kindness and Charlie V's' on the Strip by her own cunning. Pattie Primo and Vicky Vance might scream till they turned blue, but it would be to no avail. Jilly had further plans to ensure that Hollywood became her oyster. She sat up straight as a soft double brrr-brrr issued from one of the deep drawers of the desk. She quickly opened the drawer, removed a state-of-the-art encrypted phone, and unplugged an earring from her right lobe. "Yes?" She toggled a control box on the desk and a one hundred-inch plasma flat screen came to life on the wall.

"Congratulations," a man's voice purred. Jilly's eyes riveted on the screen as flashes of color zigzagged back and forth.

"I understand you have our little lady hard at work. How is she by the way?"

"Fine. She's fine."

"I expect it will take her a little while to understand the worthiness of our endeavor. That's to be expected."

"Right now I've got her thinking all we want is the screenplay. Once she begins cooperating, it'll be a small step to engage her about the program," Jilly replied.

"Yes." The voice hardened. "However, we don't have any time to waste, Jilly. With viewer sensibilities changing, we've got an almost unlimited demand for niche, special effects movies exploring new themes. Business has swelling."

The caller never appeared on screen. He was sensitive about his privacy. The screen continued to display a kaleidoscope of color, scientifically designed to thwart any interception of their conversation.

The bodiless voice continued. "With her program, we will control the future of moviemaking worldwide. Persuade her to do the right thing. You have twenty-four hours. If you fail, I will have her transferred to Mumbai. We've no time to waste."

The picture dissolved and the phone disconnected.

Jilly shivered. Everything depended on her obtaining Kate's program. Frank Primo and the Mumbai film industry had grown steadily close over the last year. Her position with Megastar had made her aware and fully involved in every shift the two men made. Primo's film with Kate's program was to have been Frank's lynch pin in an agreement with Kumar Pashagora that would have made Megastar the largest and most powerful studio in the world. Jilly spun the chair to face the window, and gazed at the Hollywood sign on the side of Mount Lee. She did not intend to see the sign changed to read Bollywood, and she would never let any interfering Hollywood agent searching for Kate to derail her.

Turning back to the desk, she picked up the phone. "Get me Hank Tolomeo. Tell him it's urgent."

Thirty seconds later Hank was on the line. "Jilly, what's up?"

"Pashagora has given me twenty-four hours to get the program, otherwise his people will take Kate back to India."

"Have you talked with her?"

"Not in person, only by computer."

"Then I suggest you get over to the vault soon as it's dark. I'll fly down tonight. If Pashagora gets his hands on her we'll never see her or the program again."

"How could he get her to India, Hank? Getting through airport security—hell, we have to take our shoes off to fly anywhere."

"Don't kid yourself. He could spirit her out of the country any moment hidden in one of his private jets. Trust me. Arrange a walk-on pass for me at the studio gate. I'll join you at the vault." He hung up before she could answer.

Chapter 25

Kate knew it was only a matter of time before someone came. Taking Rob down had no doubt triggered alarms. If she was to escape, it had to be now. She stared again at the air-conditioning duct. Surely, it must lead somewhere outside. Clambering onto one of the benches and standing on tiptoe, she could almost grasp the galvanized metal vent. She would need a tad more height to get close enough to pry open the industrial sized outlet vent. Jumping down, she looked for a chair, a box, anything to stack on the bench. She'd also need a tool to pry it off.

"You don't honestly think you can make a break for it through the air vents, do you?"

Kate jumped at the sound of the voice. Jilly was standing in the doorway.

"It might work in one of your scripts, Kate, but not in real life."

Kate didn't recognize her at first. "Who…?"

Jilly sauntered into the room. "Jilly Suede, remember me? I was at the wrap party."

Kate sighed. "You gave me a scare. Thank God you found me."

"I never lost you, Kate. I was the one who put you here."

The room seemed to tilt causing Kate to lose all sense of reality for a moment. *What is this woman saying? Why would Jilly entomb her in a film vault?*

"You did a hell of a job on Rob." Jilly indicated the hapless automaton. "Sit down, Kate. We have a lot to talk about."

Chapter 26

A trumpet-like "Yoo-hoo" from Vicky Vance cut through the din at Musso and Frank's.

Lev grimaced. "Stay close, Mel. If she asks you any questions, act dumb."

"Vicky, dear." Lev air kissed her rouged cheek, inhaling her fragrant, heady perfume.

"So glad to…" Vicky stopped in mid-sentence at the sight of Mel. "Who is this wonderful looking young man, Lev? One of your writers?"

"No. He's with Apple."

Vicky's eyes devoured Mel and she was ready for more. "Do you mean the computer company?"

"Yes, he's a friend of Kate's. They were at UCLA together."

"Does he have a name?"

"Sure. Mel, meet Vicky Vance, ace Hollywood reporter."

Vicky's mouth tightened as she took Mel's hand. "I'm very pleased to meet you, Mister…?"

"Pashagora, Melhi Pashagora"

Mel's looks, accent and last name immediately rang a bell for Vicky. Her eyes lit up.

"Don't tell me. You're the son of Kumar Pashagora, owner of Mumbai International Studios," she purred.

Mel nodded.

"Then you must be here to represent your father. He was a very good friend of Frank Primo. Poor Primo."

"Yes, my father sends by me his sincere condolences to Mrs. Primo." He glanced around the room. "Unfortunately, I haven't met her yet."

"Then you come along with me and I'll introduce you." Reaching out a thin, claw like hand she snagged Mel's sleeve and tugged him toward her. "She will be touched to know your father sent you as his emissary."

Lev snagged a proffered glass of white wine from a passing waiter and tagged along behind the twosome.

"Your father was a close friend and business associate of my husband," Pattie Primo said after introductions. "I had the pleasure of meeting him once when he came to visit Frank on business. I heard he's given up international travel."

"Yes, his age has slowed him."

"What a pity."

"It is. However, he is a keen believer in modern electronics, especially telecommunications. He says he can now travel more rapidly over the radio waves than he ever could before."

"What a wonderful attitude." Pattie turned to Lev. "Is Mel

one of your clients?"

"He's a friend of Kate's and has volunteered to help me find her."

"No one's heard from her yet?" Pattie looked alarmed.

"The police are investigating. In the meantime, Mel and I are doing our own search. Rumors fly through Hollywood faster than spam on the internet. As the word gets out that we're searching for Kate, someone will recall something we can use."

Vicky glared. "Are you insinuating that my lines of communication to the inner circle of this town are lacking?"

Lev swirled the remains of his wine. "No, Vicky, not at all." He drained his glass and nodded to Mel. "Shall we go?"

"I think you really pissed Vicious Vicky off back there," Mel said as the two walked away.

"No doubt," Lev grunted. "She'll go all out to get info on Kate now, just to spite me. Besides, how many women do you know who would attend a party hours after her husband was brutally murdered? Then again, Vicky and Charles were never very close."

A. G. Hayes

Chapter 27

A private jet turned from base to final approach above the Santa Monica airport, and Hank Tolomeo tightened his seat belt as the landing gear groaned into position. Unless Jilly got Kate's program before Pashagora's people spirited her ass to India it would be the end of TolomeoTechnics. An image of Jilly perched on the edge of the desk in the vault with Kate, white faced and tense, slumped in the office chair, ready to do whatever he and Jilly asked came to him.

"Frank said your program will transform the industry. We have to gather our forces to keep it here in America. We'll make millions. You *have* to work with us, Kate."

Kate glared, "Us? Kidnapping's not the best way to start a partnership, Jilly."

Easing off the desk, Jilly unfolded a metal chair and sat beside Kate. "You've been through a lot the last couple of days, but that's past now."

"Yeah, right," Kate snorted, "as long as I turn over my computer program. Keep it in America? Why should I share it with anyone?"

Jilly chuckled, "To remain alive, my dear."

Kate tensed. "Who's 'us'?"

"Mel's father and I," Jilly replied. "In two days time, I'll own Megastar. You're either going to be a part of the plan or dead."

Kate sat upright, a look of amazement on her face as she exclaimed, "Mel's father! Does Mel know about this?"

"No. His father insisted he know nothing."

"I don't believe Mel's dad would get involved in such a scheme." Kate pushed out of the chair. "He doesn't need money. He could buy and sell Megastar a dozen times over."

"He needs your program, Kate. There's a lot of competition in India, new companies are popping everywhere with computer expertise in movie technology."

"Then get one of them to sell their idea to you. You'll get nothing from me."

"If you don't deliver, Kate, Pashagora will take you to India and force it out of you. Either way, we'll get the program. The question is whether it will most benefit Hollywood or Bollywood."

Kate snorted. "No one can take another person against their will and transport them to India, for God's sake."

"I've been assured it can and will be done, if you refuse to cooperate."

Kate told herself this wasn't happening—it was all a bad dream. *Wrong,* she assured herself. "My program is safe and you'll never obtain it, here or in India," Kate said softly.

"Kate, Kate, Kate. We've already got you and the computer you brought with you to demonstrate your program to Primo," Jilly said, sweeping an arm toward the computer on the desk. "If we can't get what we need from you, then we can extract it from your computer."

"You can access my computer like you have, but if you try to open the program it will automatically self-destruct. It requires more than just a bio-scan of me to get around the self-destruct mechanism. You can run the program with my help, but you need a password to access the program itself and copy it."

"So, give it."

"I can't. I don't know it."

Jilly's face reddened. "Cut the bullshit!" She leapt from her chair and slapped Kate's smug face. "You want to make it hard on yourself, go ahead. But you'll suffer the consequences!"

"The pre-password is a series of thirty-six numbers and letters. I only know twelve of them," Kate said keeping her head turned to the side where Jilly's slap had pushed it. She needed the moment to regather her composure.

"Who has the rest?"

Kate knew she now had the upper hand. All her precautions were paying off. "Mel has twelve, and my father has the remaining twelve. The entire pre-password must be uploaded to Bezirbien-Uster Bank's mainframe computer in Zurich, Switzerland. A randomly generated password will be issued to me that unlocks all the program's functionality including the ability to copy it for twenty-four hours."

Jilly pushed past Kate, and turned at the iron door, her face livid with anger. "I'll have Mel brought here, then your father." She unlocked the door and left, the clanging sound heralding a new problem. Kate had no idea where her father was. She hadn't heard from him in over a year.

Chapter 28

"No, Jilly, Mel and Lev left ten minutes ago. Where are you? You were supposed be here at the reception." Vicky Vance had one ear covered as she spoke; the noise level was rising in ratio to the amount of alcohol consumed.

"He didn't say. Lev made a sarcastic crack and they left." Vicky saw Pattie waving a "come-over-here-quick" sign. "If I hear where they went, I'll let you know immediately, Jilly."

Vicky pushed her way through the crowd of tipsy grievers and joined Pattie who whispered in her ear, "Over there. Don Ames." Vicky looked in the direction of Pattie's pointing finger.

"What about him?"

"He's drunk."

"So are half the people in this place."

"Ames is very drunk and Chaz Falconer was with him when he blurted out he knew where Kate was. Chaz just told me."

"That guy would say anything to keep an audience. You know that."

"Well, Chaz was kind enough to come over and tell me."

Vicki stood on tiptoe trying to locate Chaz. If this was

true, she had a scoop.

"Where did he go?" Vicky rasped. "What did he say about Kate?"

"Chaz went to the men's room. He'll be right back; in fact, here he comes now." Chaz was the typical leading man of the twenty-first century, tall, good-looking and with an attitude that every chick should swoon when he appeared.

"This is off the record, Vicky, okay?" Chaz drawled.

"My lips remain forever sealed."

"I was going to tell Lev, but he'd left before I could get to him, so I told Pattie."

"Fine. Now go ahead tell me."

"Don't forget, he was pretty out of it. Anyway, Ames said that Kate never left the lot. She's still there somewhere, 'hidden away'."

"'Hidden away'," Vicky repeated. "What the hell does that mean?"

Chaz shrugged, "Ames suddenly realized he'd said too much and shut up."

"Did anyone else hear him say that?"

"I don't think so. I'd only been talking to him for a few minutes and wanted to get away when he blurted it out."

"Why would he say something like that?" Vicky asked.

"When Ames has somebody to talk to he likes to impress them. You are going to call the cops, right?"

"No, Chaz. I don't think an off-the-cuff statement of a drunk has-been would count with them, but thanks for the tip."

Chaz smiled, showing off his white teeth. "Remember where you heard it, Vicki."

"Of course I will, you darling man." She air kissed him and moved away. "Must be off. I was just leaving when Pattie called me over. Ta-ta."

A. G. Hayes

Chapter 29

Rob still lay next to the desk, flat on his back, a soft humming coming from somewhere deep inside his electronic circuitry. Kate wanted to remove one of his arms and use its claw to pry off the air vent cover. Grabbing the mop, she prodded Rob like a kid poking a crab. Nothing happened. She shoved harder; his metal body scraped across the concrete. Lifting one of Rob's arms, she peered under the armpit. *There must be a way to get inside this bastard*, she thought. She tried to turn him over but the little sucker was too heavy. Kate loosened her grip on the mop and straightened.

Suddenly, Rob's right arm jerked off the floor and his pincher-shaped right hand snagged the edge of her Nike, ripping the shoe from her left foot. Screaming, she jumped back as his left arm rose in the air, the claw snapping, zigzagging randomly, desperately seeking a target.

Scrambling away from the writhing robot, her foot accidentally kicked against one of the old film canisters. Scooping it up, she ran to one of the side benches and shakily pried open the can. It contained a deteriorating roll of 35-millimeter film, three quarters of it dust. Celluliod, she recalled, was prone to deterioration, but retained its flammablity, and the vault was full of film. Air conditioning meant air in/air out. *I could build a fire and the smoke would attract attention*, she thought, realizing as she thought it, that if she was discovered, she'd have died from smoke inhalation. *Shit.*

Staring at the metal entrance door, she noticed a sliver of a gap at the bottom of the door. Crossing to the entrance, she pushed one end of the film under the gape. It slid forward with no problem. If she could push enough film under the door, then light it, someone outside might see the sudden flame and smoke. But how to light it? She was torn between elation and despair when she remembered the book of matches inside the cellophane of the crumpled cigarette package. She'd replaced it in the desk drawer, so it meant having to get past Rob. There was no other way. She had to get the matches. Returning to the cube, she kicked off her remaining Nike.

Chapter 30

Lev had driven less than a mile from Musso and Frank's when his cell buzzed. It was Pattie. "What? And you didn't call the cops? The entire studio has to be searched. Right now, for God's sake!"

When Pattie explained that Vicky Vance had said the police wouldn't take any notice of a drunk's remark, Lev yelled, "Pattie! She wants the story for herself! Call the cops now. I'm on my way to Megastar. Call me back if you find out anything more!"

"What was that about?" Mel asked.

Lev barreled down Hollywood Boulevard. "Stupidity and celebrity. Pattie Primo says Vicky has a clue to Kate's whereabouts and intends to go public with it before notifying the cops."

"Did she say where Kate might be?"

"Yeah. Hidden someplace on the Megastar lot."

A. G. Hayes

Chapter 31

Hank Tolomeo was in a rented car when his cell rang. It was Jilly.

"Hank, we have a problem. Vicky Vance called and said the word was out that Kate could possibly be somewhere on the lot. She wanted a quote from me. She said she was going national with the story and asked if I'd agree to permit the police to search the studio to demonstrate cooperation with the authorities."

"What did you tell her?"

"I said yes, of course, that Megastar Studios had nothing to hide and would assist in any way possible to help find Kate."

"What?"

"Relax. I'm on the lot and I'll have her out of the vault along with the computer before any search can take place. I also told Vicky that studio security and our insurance carrier would insist on a search warrant before allowing anyone to tramp around a complex structure like a movie studio. That should buy us some time."

"Get her out of the vault fast, and be sure no one sees her. When I get there, I want Kate ready to be smuggled off the lot in my car."

"Where are you going to take her?"

"You'll know soon enough. Just get started."

Chapter 32

Two drivers with the same destination headed to Megastar studios. Lev, already on the Ventura Freeway was nearing the Barham Boulevard off-ramp, while Hank Tolomeo was stuck on surface streets, cursing the evening commuter traffic.

Jilly's mind was whirling with the events of the last few minutes. She hadn't told Hank about the special password, hoping to somehow get Mel in her grasp. All thoughts of that, however, vanished with the phone call to Hank. It was almost dark, and there was also no time to contact the bogus guard, the out of work actor who'd been only too happy to score points with Jilly Suede for doing the dirty work. She'd have to let go of the actor and Mel, and get Kate out of the vault herself.

Reaching into a desk drawer she removed a Ladysmith .44 derringer, a compact two shot weapon, and slipped it into her jacket pocket as her phone rang. She had expected Hank, but when Lev asked for personnel and car permits for himself and Mel to enter the movie lot, she couldn't believe her luck.

Lev braked at the entrance of Megastar and the guard slid open his window. "Go on in, Mr. Leventhal. Ms. Suede said go straight to her office. She's waiting for you."

"Thanks, Mike."

A generator truck parked outside stage one caused Lev to slow down, and bump over a tangle of cables snaking across the street.

"Setting up for night shooting," Lev commented to Med.

Mel nodded, "Busy night." He watched as technicians and gaffers pulled cables while stagehands yelled back and forth, moving scenery.

Jilly's intercom announced their arrival. "Send them in." Jilly indicated a couple of chairs when they entered. "Sit down. Let me bring you up to date." She verified she'd heard from Vicky, that the cops would arrive after they'd obtained a search warrant. She didn't mention her conversation with Hank. "I've ordered studio security to search the lot. It'll make for better publicity for the studio if we locate her rather than the police."

"When we were here the other day, Mel found one of Kate's earrings outside of stage four," Lev said.

Jilly stiffened. "Why didn't you tell me, Lev? I would have started a full search that very moment."

"You'd left the studio. I was told you'd taken a couple of days off."

"You're right. The shock of Frank's death and everything." Her eyes flicked to Mel. "Where exactly did you find the earring, Mel?"

"Alongside stage four."

"If someone forced her to go with them, they'd have most likely taken her toward the back lot," Lev added.

"From that point, they would pass the old film vaults," Jilly said. "You don't think it at all likely…" She delivered her lines like a pro and Lev and Mel seemed to fall for it.

"Still, it would be a good place to start," Lev suggested.

Jilly yanked open desk drawers, saying, "There used to be a set of dupe keys for each vault. Yes, here they are." She held up a bunch of old-fashioned keys. "It must be fifty years since they were last used." She blew imaginary dust from the tangled bunch.

Lev darted a glance at Mel, wide-eyed, perhaps thinking the earring might be the clue to finding Kate.

She jangled the keys. "Let's go."

"Maybe we should have security join us," Lev added.

"No need. We can handle this," Jilly said.

A. G. Hayes

Chapter 33

Rob was once again as still as an empty suit of armor. Kate approached the damaged robot with caution, carrying the empty film can. Eyeing the distance between herself and Rob, she took careful aim and rolled the empty reel like a hoop toward him. The reel spun across the floor without a waver and struck Rob in the side. Rob's arm struck with the swiftness of an aggressive snake and flattened it. It happened so fast, it was almost a blur. The stubby android couldn't see, but its other sensors were as sensitive as ever.

Picking two more reels off one of the racks, she placed them a safe distance from Rob. Carefully snatching her jacket from the office chair, she added it to the reels.

Taking a deep breath she lobbed her loosely balled jacket and watched it arc toward Robs chest. Again Rob's lightning-fast reaction snagged the coat in midair, the claw gripping and waving it like a flag causing the material to crack like a ship's sail in a windstorm. Then she rolled one of the reels towards him. Harsh grinding sounds of tin on concrete assured her the other arm had also gone into action.

While Rob was thus engaged, she reached carefully forward and rummaged through the drawer until she found the matches. Retreating, she glanced at the vent. She was certain that once she got the grill off, she could squirm into the duct and hopefully find her way out.

Walking barefoot around the desk on Rob, she glanced toward the bathroom and saw a mop bucket. Grabbing it, she cranked on the faucet; again, a slow trickle of rusty water. *Not fast enough,* she thought.

Walking back to the desk, she carefully grabbed the metal folding chair Jilly had left. Hefting it, she whispered in her mind, *Heavy duty. Perfect.* Grabbing its back, she swung the legs hard against the rusted tap, snapping the faucet off the washbasin and causing water to gush up to the ceiling. Snatching up the mop bucket, she held it under the water bouncing off the ceiling. Within seconds, the bucket was brim full and she dragged back to the desk, where Rob was still waving the jacket and hammering away at the film can.

Focusing on the gaping hole where his video eye had been, she held the bucket handle, and slowly began to swing the bucket back and forth, getting the feel, balancing the weight, eyeing the target—the jagged hole where the eye used to be.

Focusing all her concentration, she took a deep breath and launched the bucket. It flew in a low arc tilting forward as it neared the target. The bucket was upside down as it crashed onto Rob's head, releasing the contents into the hole where the robot's eye had been. Blue flashes shot outward, followed by sparking, sizzling and the smell of burning circuit boards. A second burst of sparks, then silence. In his death agony, the arm holding her coat had become detached and lay beside the blackened metal body. Kate picked up the folding chair and heaved it across the room where it landed squarely across his chest. Nothing. Rob was history.

Kate smiled wickedly, walked over, picked up Rob's arm. She now had the tool she needed to remove the grill.

A. G. Hayes

Chapter 34

The trio passed stage four and continued toward the absolute blackness of the back lot.

"You found the earring around this area?" Jilly asked Mel.

"Yes, over there, next to the wall."

"Stage four's the last main building before the back lot," Jilly said, switching on a large flashlight. "There's nothing much back there except an old western set and some old film vaults."

A flash of light momentarily lit up the night sky, then dimmed and was gone.

"What the hell was that?" Lev asked.

Jilly knew the flash had come from the vicinity of the vaults, and quickly said, "Most likely the security search party."

The vaults, similar to military bunkers, were built underground, and had concrete steps leading down to a metal door entrance. Only the concrete domed tops of the structures were visible above ground. Jilly knew Kate was in the nearest of the vaults where the flash had appeared.

Jilly shone the flashlight beam down the flight of steps. "Be careful," she warned, noting the pile of melted celluloid in front of the door. She had the preselected key in hand. She wanted her visitors inside. Fast.

"What's that odor?" Mel asked.

"Smells like burnt plastic," Lev replied as Jilly unlocked and pushed the metal door open.

"Whew! It smells different in here. Much stronger." Lev stopped when he saw the desk underneath the overhead lamp, smoke emanating from behind it.

Jilly shut the door, her right hand gripping the Ladysmith in her pocket. She registered mock surprise, saying, "What the hell?"

"Hi-tech squatters?" asked Lev, as he approached the work desk. "What do you make of it Mel?"

"That's Kate's computer!"

Mel plugged it and the yellow cable into the laptop and tapped a few keys. "This unit is now a slave, and only able send and receive to one other computer."

Lev leaned in. "You mean, like an intercom?"

"Good analogy, Lev. That's exactly what it does."

Jilly fumed. If Hank had arrived sooner, they'd have had these meddlesome fools tied up and the place locked down permanently. But more important, where was Kate?

"We should lock up and wait for the police, Lev. This is a possible crime scene," Jilly suggested. A quick survey told her Kate was gone. All she wanted to do now was get out of the vault before Hank came on the scene and blew both their covers. "I'll go outside and call security. My cell doesn't work in here. You two stay and see what else you can find." She handed the flashlight to Lev and left. The longer she and Hank could remain innocent bystanders, the better.

Lev watched her leave. "Okay, let's check out the rest of this place, but do it carefully. As Jilly said, this is a possible crime scene."

Jilly hit Hank's number as she hurriedly made her way across the back lot. "Hank! Come straight to my office and stay away from the vaults! I have no idea where the hell Kate is."

Pushing a side door open, Lev entered the cramped sleeping quarters and saw an unmade cot with items of women's clothing tossed across it, and on the floor beside the cot, a single Nike running shoe.

"Mel, get in here!"

"Those are Kate's clothes," Mel confirmed and paled. "She must be here somewhere."

Exiting the sleeping room, they were stopped by a heap of scorched electronic gear.

"Whoa, what's that?" Lev asked, pointing the beam onto the metal heap that had once been Rob.

Mel gave a low whistle. "TolomeoTechnics builds those." Slowly he walked around the broken robot. "I've seen this model at the plant in Palo Alto." He pushed his foot against the remaining arm. "This guy looks as if he was hit with mortar fire."

"Hank Tolomeo's company manufactures those?"

"Sure, among other things. Wonder what happened to his other arm?"

"Hank Tolomeo makes robots."

"He's been into robotics for several years. It's a fast growing industry. They use them, dolled up to look human, in place of stunt men. The government loves them, too."

"I bet." Together, they searched the semidarkness of the vault, Lev swinging the flashlight beam side to side, as they passed rack after rack of the stored film reels.

A mutilated grill cover lay on a bench and next to it Rob's missing arm. Lev gazed up into at the open duct. "I think I know where Kate went."

Chapter 35

"What?" Franz Villand rasped into the phone.

"Kate's escaped from the vault," Ames said.

"You gotta' be kidding!"

"I'm not."

"I sat by that phone at K-Mart three mornings in a row and no one told me." Villand's voice quavered. "I told you I didn't like this."

"First our boss, then Hank Tolomeo called. We're supposed to find her. She's running loose some place on the Megastar back lot. I'll pick you up at your place." A dial tone droned in Villand's ear.

Villand hung up, his lips tightening. He went into the men's room and stared into the mirror. Within seconds, there was no sign of worry or concern on the face reflected back. In fact, his eyes had taken on steely glint as he said aloud, "It's show time."

A. G. Hayes

Chapter 36

Outside the vault, Lev's flashlight beam picked out an industrial air conditioning unit sitting in the shadows. One side of the unit sagged open on a broken hinge. Studio security swarmed around it.

Lev whispered to Mel, "Exit Kate Keenan." In the distance, he could see the moving lights of other search parties. "More studio cops," he added. "By the time the Burbank Police get a search warrant, any clues will be trampled."

In the distance, a police siren warbled its approach and Mel said, "Kate's going to have find a way to make it off the lot."

"She could head for the night shoot," Lev said. "Hide in full view with a clipboard and a smile, and easily merge with the rest of the crew. Wait! Here comes Jilly and Hank."

Jilly and Hank joined the studio security standing outside the vault entrance.

"There was no one in the vault, Ms. Suede," a grizzled captain reported. "We've searched everywhere. There was a pile of burnt electronic gear and the air conditioning grill was knocked off. A small person could have squirmed through."

"Did your people check where the AC entrance and exit

points are for that vault?"

The burly old captain bit his tongue. He'd served twenty-five years with the Los Angeles Police Department before serving eight more with the studio. His sour expression betrayed his dislike at having to report to a civilian, especially a bitch like Jilly Suede.

"Yes, Ma'am, we did. The door on one of the surface units was hanging open. She could've made it out. I have a party working the area."

"Keep me informed, Captain." Jilly and Hank remained silent until the captain had moved away.

Hank muttered, "Bloody Keystone Kops!"

Jilly hissed, "Let's get back to my office. If you'd have arrived sooner, we could have had Kate in our hands and Lev tied up and locked away forever."

"Mel and I will stay with security, if it's okay with you Jilly," Lev called out from the group of security men near the vault.

"Appreciate it Lev," Jilly called back. "Let's stay in touch."

Hank crossed to the portable bar in Jilly's office and poured two fingers of single malt.

"I told you what Pashagora said on the phone," Jilly said curtly. "He's going to have his people haul her off to India, and if you mess with Mel, he'll include us. Mumbai doesn't sound like my kind of place."

Hank sipped his drink. "I've alerted Ames and Villand. They're coming on the lot to help in the search."

"Hank, studio security and police are already swarming the place. What good will those two idiots do?"

"Kate knows them and will trust them."

A. G. Hayes

Chapter 37

Villand answered the door with the chain latched; his eyes glittered as he squinted through the gap.

Ames grunted, "Come on, get moving. We don't have all night."

Closing the door behind them, Villand, dressed in blue jeans, a dark gabardine windbreaker and a baseball cap pulled low over his eyes followed Ames to the car.

"What's the moustache for, Villand?" Ames asked as he switched on the ignition. "One of your 'thousand faces'?"

"I feel better in disguise. I don't want anyone on the set to recognize me."

Ames sniggered. "I wouldn't worry, the last time you were on a working set was so long ago, whoever was there will be in the Motion Picture Home for the Aged."

Villand smoothed the moustache, "Thanks a lot."

A. G. Hayes

Chapter 38

Pressing back into the deep shadows cast by a saloon on the western set, Kate heard then saw search party flashlights swing from side to side in the blackness. All she had to do was walk toward them, call out, and it would be over. A chill trickled down her spine. More likely, she would be safe only for as long as it took someone to abduct her again.

The threat from Jilly Suede that she could end up a prisoner in India caused her to linger in the shadows. She needed help, but who could she trust? Was Mel part of the plan? They were engaged to be married. The plan was get married in America, then, in time, go meet his father. Jilly may well have been lying regarding Mel's father being any part of the kidnapping. Her mind spun. Flashlights again pierced the dark air, this time closer. She must get off the lot.

A. G. Hayes

Chapter 39

Jilly and Hank walked onto the sound stage just as John Bizet, the director called cut. The high-powered spots dimmed, and the set lighting brightened as stagehands began preparing for the next set up. The director saw Jilly and waved.

"I'm surprised to see you, Jilly. What's up?"

"I came by to give you a heads up. There's a search on for the woman who went missing at the wrap party the other night. Police are involved. I'll ask them to wait until you finish this shoot. How much longer do you figure?"

Bizet looked surprised. "You mean Kate Keenan, the writer?"

"Yes, but it could be a false alarm."

"No problem, Jilly. We should be through in about a half hour. We've just one more short scene and we're done."

Jilly indicated Hank. "You two have met I take it?"

Hank offered a hand to the director. "Sure, good to see you again, John. It's been awhile."

Jilly scanned the set for signs of Kate while the two men chatted. Finding none, she remarked, "Come on, Hank, we don't want to hold up production."

Bizet turned back to half a dozen antsy assistants waiting to ask questions.

"I saw Ames, but not Villand," Jilly said as they walked carefully through a maze of cables strewn across the sound stage floor.

"He's here," Hank said.

Jilly grabbed Hank's arm. "Damn! Look who's butting in again."

Hank turned in the direction of her gaze and saw Lev and Mel standing inside the entrance.

"No problem," Hank said. "Let's go over and talk with them."

"Are you crazy?"

Hank chuckled. "Your guilty conscience is showing, my dear. They know nothing."

Squaring her shoulders, Jilly walked over to Lev and Mel. "Hank suggested we alert the night shoot to expect an interruption."

Lev gave a terse nod. "Did you expect Kate to be here?"

Hank cut in. "No. John Bizet, the director was at the wrap party and I thought we'd ask if he'd seen Kate."

"Had he?"

"No. But it was worth a try." Hank indicated they should move outside. "I thought you were going to work with security."

"And I thought you'd gone back to Palo Alto. We decided to search on our own. If it was Kate locked in the vault, we know how she escaped," Lev said.

All at once, Mel blurted. "Then she's somewhere on the lot!"

"Likely she's left the studio by now and is contacting the police," Lev added.

Jilly's face blanched at the thought. She clutched Hank's arm. "Her kidnappers will likely hunt her down again. This is terrible. She might make for your place, Mel."

"Possible. Maybe I should get back there," Mel said, glancing at Lev.

"I'll drop you off," Lev muttered.

"I'll stay with Hank," Jilly said quickly. "If we hear anything I'll call you at once."

A. G. Hayes

Chapter 40

Kate was remained inside the saloon, but was standing in the deep shadows, peering through the slats of the batwing saloon doors. She was sure she'd heard something, but could see only blackness. Moving to one side, she bumped against a table and knocked over a chair. She caught the curved back before it clattered to the floor, then she heard the sound again. Gripping the chair, she held it over her head ready to clobber who ever came through the door.

A lone man pushed open the right hand swing door and Kate brought the chair down hard, smashing the top of the door. Splinters flew and Villand leapt to one side. Had he pushed open the left batwing, he'd have had his head split widc open.

Kate's arms tingled from the force of the blow.

"Jesus! Kate! I came to help you. Take it easy."

"Franz, is that you? What's with the mustache?"

"You almost killed me."

"What are you doing creeping around the back lot? I thought you were one of them."

"Them?"

"The scum bags who held me in the film vault."

"Everyone's searching for you," Villand lied. "That's why I'm here."

Kate lowered the remains of the chair. "How did you find me?"

"Lucky guess. I was trailing along behind the security search team. Some of us from the wrap party volunteered to help."

"Thanks."

"You're safe now. No one can hurt you."

"Yeah, right," she said bitterly, thinking, *where have I heard that before?*

"Come with me. I'll take you to Jilly Suede's office"

Kate had decided she didn't care for the Man of a Thousand Faces after meeting him at the wrap party, and now that she was again face-to-face with him, she liked him even less. "I want off the lot, as far away as possible," she replied. No way was she going to trust this quirky cretin and have Jilly get her hands on her again.

Still, her inclination was to play along and follow him until she had an opportunity to dump him and go solo. Creeping along behind his skinny ass, she removed the steel finger she'd broken off of Rob's claw hand from her pocket.

"Okay," Villand said agreeably. "Let's go."

Chapter 41

"Where exactly are we going?" Mel asked, as Lev turned right out of the studio gate onto Barham Boulevard, continued for a block, then made a second right turn.

"Back into the studio through gate three," Lev replied.

"I thought we were going to my place in case Kate showed up there."

"That's what I wanted Jilly and Hank to believe."

"What's going on, Lev?"

"Listen, I have a hunch Jilly and Hank have something to do with Kate's disappearance."

"Jilly and Hank?" Mel exclaimed. "Why do you think that?"

"Remember when we first entered the film vault and found Kate's computer?" Mel nodded. "Well, Jilly suddenly became agitated. She couldn't wait to get out of the vault to call the cops."

"Oh, yes, and we found the robot from Hank's company in the vault along with Kate's clothes," Mel said, his eyes squinting as if thinking it through. "But I've known Hank for some time. Why would he want to kidnap Kate?"

"I don't know. I could be wrong, but in the meantime,

we're going back on the lot to continue our search, starting with the night shoot on stage one," Lev said.

A walk-on permit authorized by security was good for all Megastar's studio gates. He was going to secretly reenter the studio at a side entrance, gate three, a lesser entrance used mainly by trades people and studio transport.

Chapter 42

"Once Kate contacts the police, it'll all be over," Jilly's voice quavered.

"I have no intention of allowing her to contact anyone, Jilly," Hank rasped, removing his cell phone from his pocket. "Where are you?" he ordered and turned away from Jilly to listen to the voice of Ames telling him he was still on stage one. "Well, get out of there. Right now. Go over to Shoreham drive and stake out Mel's place. I think Kate's heading for the Pashagora apartment. She's not on the lot."

"You want me to locate Villand first?"

"No, get over to the apartment now. No time to waste. I'll call him."

Villand's cell vibrated and he stopped, Kate bumping into him in the darkness.

"Yeah?" he whispered, glancing nervously at Kate.

"Get over to Shoreham drive," Hank commanded, "and meet Ames. Kate's off the lot."

"What are you talking about? She's right here beside me, I found her, and I'm bringing her in."

Kate gripped Rob's metal finger tighter, but the angle wasn't right. Her foot rattled against a rock as she sidestepped away from Villand. Instantly, she scooped it up; it was heavy, and fit into her hand as if tailor-made. Without hesitation, she hit him at the base of his skull. He went down without a sound.

She patted the ground, trying to find the cell phone in the darkness. When she found the phone, she heard Hank's voice calling Villand's name. She disconnected, and tapped Mel's number.

Lev and Mel had passed through gate three without problem, and were driving toward stage one when Mel's cell chirped.

"Kate! Where are you?"

Lev immediately braked to a stop. "Give me the phone." Kate brought him quickly up to date to the moment Villand hit the ground.

"I'm near the western set, and I can see flashlight beams in the distance," she whispered.

"Good. Listen carefully: Stay right where you are. I'll contact security and they'll come and get you."

Kate shot back, "No way Lev. They'll get me and take me to Jilly. She's the person responsible for my kidnapping."

"Good God! In that case, go back to the western set and lay low. Mel and I will be there in less than five minutes to pick you up."

"Lev, there's a search party heading toward me. I told

you, I can see their flashlights."

"Then hide! They'll see Villand and take him to security. When they leave, run back to the saloon."

"Yes but…" The phone suddenly went dead.

Parking the car, Lev and Mel hurried in the direction of the western set. The evening was moonless, and the back lot encompassed in absolute darkness.

Kate stuffed the cell phone into her pocket. The moving lights were getting closer, and she could hear voices calling to each other. She had to hide. Glancing to her right, she saw a mass of old scenery silhouetted against the glow from the night shoot. Within seconds, she was amidst the wood and canvas, crouched low as the search party came upon Villand sprawled on the ground. It happened the way Lev said. They picked up Villand and carried him toward the sound stage, leaving the way clear for her to head back to the saloon.

Lev and Mel were standing in the shadows on the wooden sidewalk next to the saloon when Kate slinked by. Lev saw her first. "We're here Kate! Come on," he whispered urgently.

Less than five minutes later, with Kate curled on the floor under a blanket behind the front seat of Lev's car, the three exited the gate.

Lev waved to the guard as he drove off the lot. "Okay, Kate you can come up for air now."

A. G. Hayes

Chapter 43

Studio security called half way through Jilly's second gin and tonic. Her face paled as she asked, "When?"

Hank scooped up an extension, and heard security tell Jilly they'd found Frank Villand unconscious near the western set. He was now in the studio hospital.

Jilly slammed the phone down. "I don't believe this! That little bitch is going to ruin everything."

"Order security to stop all traffic entering or leaving the studio. Also, find out if Leventhal cleared the lot. We need to be sure if he left."

Jilly dialed security.

"Mr. Leventhal left through the main gate at seven fifty-five." There was a pause, and the security guard continued. "Seems he returned to the lot through gate three at eight-oh-two and left again at eight-fifty," she said to Hank.

Jilly hung up. "Lev got her off the lot, Hank. Contact Mumbai and alert Pashagora."

A. G. Hayes

Chapter 44

Lev drove straight to his place on Lookout Mountain. He'd decided they should stay together, keep away from Shoreham and plan their next move. Kate didn't want to go to the cops, fearing the media would become involved and turn everything into a circus.

Sitting at the kitchen table, Kate finished a bowl of Lev's homemade spaghetti.

"Like more?" he asked.

"No, I ate too much already. Good pasta, Lev."

"Leftovers always taste better. I made that two days ago."

"Better than the slop that scumbag in the vault served."

"You two both need a good night's sleep. Come on. I'll show you your rooms." When they stood, Lev continued, "It's so good to have you here," he said, giving Kate a brief, but substantial hug. He shook Mel's hand with a smile, "Sleep well."

Fifteen minutes later, the house was silent. He must decide his next move. He decided to make a list of the players and mark which ones might know his home address.

A. G. Hayes

Chapter 45

Hank Tolomeo returned to his Palo Alto plant and chaired an emergency meeting of his board of directors, bringing them up to date on Kate's program, and his intention that TolomeoTechnics obtain it. His ferret-black eyes flicked across the faces of the men sitting at the long, polished teak conference table.

Hank Tolomeo had come a long way since he'd earned a living repairing television sets in Hollywood back in the late fifties. Tolomeo had taken out a loan on his modest house in the San Fernando Valley, offered a job to the smartest technician in the company and started a small electronics lab in what later became Silicone Valley. His technician turned out to be a whiz kid with the new craze device called a computer. His two-man operation grew lightening fast and both men made millions.

Mr. Tolomeo held up a boney hand. "We're talking billions here. MGM, Paramount, Warner Brothers, to name a few, would love to know what I know about her program."

Tolomeo turned the pages of a thick ledger on his desk. "And we mustn't forget Bollywood." Hank was a man of power, with an alpha ego, driven by an insatiable inner force to control the film and mass media market. What Kate had written was his taste of honey, and he sought it with an urgency bordering on lunacy.

Tolomeo leaned forward. "This meeting is over, people." A florid faced man wanting more details objected. "Relax, Jonathan, I'm meeting a few friends in LA tomorrow. We'll get the girl and the program, and I'll have everything wrapped up in twenty-four hours."

Chapter 46

"Believe me, Stace, I rarely do this," Lev whispered. He was sitting in the Adirondack chair on the deck, a cell phone pressed to his ear.

A sleepy voice answered. "You know what time it is Lev?"

"That's what I mean. I hardly ever call anyone this late at night."

"It's *morning*, Lev. Very early morning. What's up? And why are you whispering."

"I'm outside on my deck."

"Fine and I'm fully awake with the light on. This better be good."

"Kate is here at my place."

"You found her! Where was she?" Stacy was now wide-awake. "Does anyone else know you have her?"

"Yes, I'm afraid they do."

"What's that mean?" asked Stace slowly.

"Trouble," Lev whispered. "At the least, Kate's life is again in danger. She was held in a film vault on the lot at Megastar."

"Have you've been drinking, Lev?"

"Not since lunch with you. And get this: Hank Tolomeo and Jilly Suede were part of the plot. Can you drive up here right now? I can go over everything with you then. One other thing, don't tell a soul. Kate's life may depend on it."

"Put a pot of coffee on, Lev. I'm on my way."

Lev switched off, patted his pocket to be sure Al Jolson was still okay, and then went inside to make coffee.

A few minutes later, Stacy Hart was squinting at Lev over the rim of a steaming mug of coffee. "You can't keep Kate hidden up here forever."

"I know, and I don't intend to. I'm going to hustle Kate and Mel out of town for a few days."

"Okay, then what?"

Lev sipped his coffee thoughtfully before saying, "That'll be up to you, Stace."

"Me?"

"Okay, maybe I should have asked if you help first"

This was a first for Stacy. In all her years as a publicist, no one had ever asked her to abet in getting anyone *out* of town.

"You hide Kate and Mel and I do what?"

"Pretend you don't know where we are while keeping your ears and eyes open for any reactions among those who were at the wrap party."

"I see. You want me to act dumb and play spy."

"Well, yes, if you want to put it that way."

"Okay," Stace agreed. "And if I see or hear anything, then what?"

"I'll call you at least once a day."

"Lev, despite Kate's concern about turning this into a media circus, it might be best to report this all to the police. A whole lot safer, too."

"Yeah, I know, but she has her mind made up. Besides, she wants to see her father. She says it's important."

Stacy sputtered, "Her father? I didn't know she had one. I thought she was brought up by her grandparents."

"She was, Stace. It's a long story. Will you do it, play the dumb spy?"

Stace brightened, "On one condition, Lev."

"What's that?"

"When it's all over, I get to be Kate's publicist."

"I guarantee it, Stace."

A. G. Hayes

Chapter 47

Stace drove Lev to a car rental agency in Hollywood.

"Call me every day, Lev."

He watched her drive off, rented a car and headed home. The sky was turning from dark to pink when he pulled into his driveway, recalling the old saying, "Red sky in the morning, sailors warning."

His car was in the garage, making anyone interested think he was there. The rental would lessen the chance of anyone recognizing him when they drove away.

Lev roused Kate and Mel; they entered the kitchen complaining about needing fresh clothes. Lev poured them coffee and said they could buy some later in the day.

"Where are we going?" Kate asked.

"Away. You didn't want the cops to help, so it's up to me."

"Do you think it's wise to vanish, Lev?"

"In this case, yes. You saw the way Hank Tolomeo and Jilly Suede acted. They're playing for keeps."

Mel looked tired. "I've known Hank for some time and I never dreamed he'd be a part of a plan to kidnap Kate."

"Yeah, well, it's hard to know people today, Mel. Finish your coffee. I want an early start. Kate, any idea where your dad is right now?"

"When I last spoke to him a year ago, he was in Arizona."

Lev frowned. "Nothing since?"

"No. He was "going hermit" as he called it. He was start-ing a new book."

"Where in Arizona was he last time you spoke?"

"Flagstaff. But, like I said, he was going hermit." Kate crinkled her forehead. "Wait a minute. He said something about heading to some desolate place called Dolan Springs. He'd chosen it because it had small local library with a couple of public computers with internet access."

"Doesn't your Dad use a computer?"

"Yes, he does, but without internet service?" Kate shrugged her shoulders. "Anyway, I remember he said he was going to rent a trailer." She paused, "Wait, I have an idea."

Kate returned to the kitchen with her laptop.

"I didn't know you had that. I thought you'd left it in the vault."

"The one in the vault was compromised. Just before I left, the self-destruct program did it in. This is yours, silly."

She flipped the lid open, booted up and Googled "Library, Dolan Springs, Arizona."

"Here we go. There's a Skype phone number. It's too early to phone, but it shows we can Fax to this number even when they're closed."

Kate typed, "IMPORTANT! Call me as soon as you receive this. Collect if necessary. It's a matter of life and death." She inserted her name and cell number and hit FAX. Within seconds, it was on its way and they were ready to fly out the door.

"I'll need to stop briefly to pick up my spare computer. It's a duplicate of the one that was destroyed. Is that okay?"

Lev nodded his approval.

"In that case, I'll stay behind to collect and pack some necessities. When you've got the computer, swing by and we can load up and leave.

Thirty minutes later, the three were back at Lev's house. Kate slipped her secret second computer into a carrying case Lev provided and slung it over her shoulder like a tourist in a bad neighborhood. "It's part of me," she explained. "You still have Al Jolson, right Lev?"

"Yeah," Lev answered, "'Never leave home without it'." Lev glanced around and noticed that Mel wasn't in the room. He also noted that Kate hadn't mentioned Al Jolson in front of her fiancé. He frowned.

A. G. Hayes

Chapter 48

Ethan Keenan was sipped his first cup of coffee of the day when he heard a snuffling sound outside of his trailer. Still in his shorts and tee shirt, he tugged open the warped front door.

A shaggy haired, tongue-lolling mutt sat on a shabby doormat. The word "Welcome" had worn off long before Ethan moved in.

"Morning, Yellow Dog," Ethan growled.

"Ethan, do you have a daughter?" A loud voice rang out from across the trailer park as a large woman appeared from within a large cloud of cigarette smoke and waddled toward him.

"Who wants to know, Judith?"

"The library lady." Judith was almost at the front door and Yellow Dog slunk into the shadow of the trailer.

Judith was short of breath most every day and hefting herself the twenty feet from her battered Airstream had left her gasping. "Well, do you?"

"Yeah, she lives in California."

Judith took a deep suck on her cigarette and rasped, "Urgent message. C'mon."

Ethan followed her across the dusty lot to her trailer where she pointed to a phone—a black rotary job at least thirty years old. "The library lady's on the line."

Ethan picked up and answered, "Yes it is." He looked around for something to write on. Judith, reading his mind, turned over a store receipt and pushed it along with a stub of a pencil across the tabletop. "Okay, give me the number." He jotted the number on the piece of paper, thanked the woman at the library, and hung up.

"Not bad news, I hope."

"Don't know yet. I have to call this number to find out."

Judith had taken over managing the trailer park after her husband died in an accident on the interstate outside of Phoenix. That had been nineteen years ago. She knew everything about everyone in the park with the exception of Ethan. All she knew about him was that he kept to himself and paid his rent on time.

"Use the phone again. I'll wait outside."

"Thanks, Judith." He waited until the screen door had creaked shut, then dialed the number, remembering when phones took this long to crank.

Kate answered on the third ring, "Dad?"

"What's up?" he asked. "You okay?"

"I'm fine, but I have a problem. Mel and I are on the run. Jilly Suede and Hank Tolomeo are after me and my computer program. They want to steal the movie program. Jilly threatened I would be hijacked to India and forced to give the program to them. I told them that even if they did, I couldn't give them the program as I didn't have the password."

"Whoa, whoa, Baby. Slow down. How did you find me?" Ethan asked.

"I remembered you saying you were going to 'hermit away' in a place called Dolan Springs out in the desert. You mentioned there was a library. I left a message with the library and they called me back, telling me a person of your description used one of their computers at least once a week. You didn't have a card, never mentioned your name or where you lived, but the librarian said that if anyone in the area knew you, it would be Judith out at the trailer park."

"So much for being a desert recluse," Ethan muttered. "Jilly Suede and Hank Tolomeo. So they know about our password arrangement?"

"Yes, I told Jilly I didn't have the full thirty-six alpha-numeric combination and I had no idea where you were."

"Did she believe you?"

"I think so, but I bet Tolomeo is arranging to locate you as we speak."

"Great," Ethan said sarcastically.

"Lev suggested we three should meet in Las Vegas and talk over the situation."

"Who's Lev?"

"My new agent. Listen, Dad. Can you meet us in Vegas? You do have a car, don't you?"

"Of course, I do. Where in Vegas and when?"

Kate consulted Lev, then shot back, "Binion's Gambling Hall and Hotel, one-hundred-twenty-eight East Freemont Street."

"Why there? You own stock in the place?" Ethan asked.

"No. Lev just pushed the yellow pages in front of me and tapped their ad. It's downtown. Lots of people. A good place to vanish. Joanie, that's his secretary, will book four rooms in her name. What do you think?"

"I'll pack a bag. What name are we booked under?"

"Malone. Joanie Malone. She's prepaying with her credit card and I'll have it with me. Our names won't be used."

"Okay, Kate, I'll leave in the next half hour. Vegas is seventy-five miles away, so I should be on Freemont Street in less than three hours. Where are you now?"

"Don't rush, Dad. We're still in LA. Meet us at six this evening in the foyer of Binion's. Wear a red carnation."

Ethan hung up. *She still had a sense of humor, my gal*, he thought and smiled.

Ethan told Judith he would be away for a couple of days, and if anyone came asking where he was, to tell them she had no idea.

"That's easy. I really don't know," Judith said.

"Right. Be sure to give Yellow Dog his bacon rind every morning."

A. G. Hayes

Chapter 49

Jilly Suede was well aware that the murders of Frank Primo and Charles Vance, two men who had been close friends and business associates for many years, would, eventually put her in the circle of suspects. When the reading of his Will revealed Jilly as heir to Frank's fortune, the circle would tighten considerably.

Jilly had made certain that Frank's doctor, a man he'd seen at least once a month, wrote the death certificate showing the cause of death as a heart attack. There was no autopsy and Frank had gone out the way he wanted to—cremation.

Charlie Vance's departure from earth, murdered with a knife between his shoulder blades after singing a hymn in church, was altogether a different story, and Kate being on the run made everything worse. Should she tell the police of her incarceration in the film vault? Or would remain silent, knowing the possibility of she herself being shanghaied to India if she wasn't successful in recapturing Kate. Both Hank and Jilly knew Kate had to be located and temporarily coerced into silence, no matter what it took.

Glancing at her watch, Jilly gauged that Hank would be arriving in the next few minutes. She had grown comfortable sitting behind Frank's large desk, and everyone at the studio took it for granted she'd remain in charge until further notice. Her phone rang.

"Hank, I thought you'd be here by now."

"Running a little late," Hank said, "I want you to meet me at the Mexican Place, say in half an hour. I booked our usual booth in the back. We'll have dinner and I'll bring you up to date."

Jilly hung up. There would come a time, soon she hoped, when Hank would be out of her life. He was getting too damned bossy.

A half hour later, Jilly slid into the red leather booth she and Hank always used. The server, seeing her, smiled and called her by name. "Evening Ms. Suede, we alone tonight?"

"No Fran, I'm a little early. Mr Tolomeo will be here soon."

Fran nodded, "Two glasses of white wine as usual?"

"Sure Fran. On second thought, bring a carafe. We'll order later." Fran set two leather-covered menus on the table and left.

How long ago was it when she and Hank had first come to the Mexican Place? That's what they called it, never by its correct name, just the Mexican Place. It must have been two years at least. The restaurant was located opposite the main gate of Megastar and served delicious food, good house wine, and, for Hank and Jilly, pleasant times.

Fran returned and set an empty wine glass and a carafe of white on the table, along with a glass of the same for Jilly.

"We were all so sad to hear about Mr Primo. He was a wonderful man."

Jilly sipped, and then smiled sadly saying, "Yes, we all miss him terribly." Fran shook her head, and backed away from the table leaving Jilly with her own thoughts.

"Sorry, I'm late." Hank slid next to Jilly, filled his glass and drank half of it in one gulp. "I needed that. No news on where they went yet. I have a top crew working on it."

"Who are they?" Jilly asked.

"No one you know. Trust me, they're good."

"So is a thirty-six digit password, Hank."

"Yeah, but don't worry. We'll get her, her father and Mel."

"Does Mel's father know they're on the run?"

"Yes, I talked to him today."

Jilly swirled her wine, took a sip and asked, "And?"

"Mr Pashagora is very unhappy. He advised me that unless we found them in the next twenty-four hours he would send some of his own people over from Mumbai."

Jilly checked the time. "Oh boy, let's order before I loose what's left of my appetite."

A. G. Hayes

Chapter 50

Ethan parked his car and approached the main entrance of Binion's. It was two minutes to six. As expected, Freemont Street was ablaze with neon and filled with crowds. Lev had been right, it was a good place to hide in full view.

Suddenly, seemingly from out of nowhere, Kate was beside him, her arms flung around his neck. "Dad, you look too thin."

Ethan felt a surge of joy go through him; he hadn't realized how much he'd missed her. "Wow, baby you look great. Now tell me what this is all about."

Kate linked arms with him and they entered the lobby. She pointed. "First, let's meet Lev, and you know Mel. There they are."

They walked over to meet the two men; she made the introductions.

"Nice to meet you, Lev. Good to see you Mel," Ethan said, and then asked, "Can we find a quiet spot where you can fill me in on what's going on?"

Lev flicked his eyes upward, "My room's as good as any. Come on."

Kate sat in the only chair and the three men sat on the bed

facing her. Kate quickly brought her father up to date, ending with, "So, we left town and came here. Lev will check in with Stacy Hart every day. She'll give us a report on what's happening."

Ethan asked Lev, "Is that the same Stacy Hart I'm thinking about?"

"Stace has been in town a long time. You might have known her from your days in Hollywood."

Ethan nodded, "Publicity, right?"

"Yeah, she has her own place now. I can trust her to help us. Like Kate said, we'll be in touch with each other at least once a day."

"What are the chances you were followed here, or someone knew you were coming to meet me?"

"Slim, I'd say. Stacy won't know where we are until I phone her later," Lev said.

Ethan stood up, walked across to the window, and looked down at the activity below. "I suggest you don't call Stacy, Lev."

Lev frowned. "You mean you don't trust her?"

"If you've made it out of town without being tailed, we should leave it at that for now."

Mel tapped his fingers on his knee. "Now that we're all together, we should pool our password numbers and contact the Bezirbien-Uster Bank in Zurich."

"That would be foolish," Ethan rasped. "The program is safe. We don't want them to catch us with the computer and the password, do we?"

"Good point, Dad. When the time comes for us to share the program, we can contact Zurich."

Ethan grinned. "Good girl. Now, this place is famous for a good steak. How about we find a dark corner in the dining room and see how good they really are?"

Lev heaved off the bed and rubbed his lower back. "I agree, however, one stop before the dining room. First, we get a wig for Kate."

A short time later, a young brunette and three men were eating dessert in the dining room. "Been awhile since I ate so well. And they're right. A great steak," Ethan declared.

"The first thing I said to you, Dad, was that you were too thin. Must be your desert diet."

"You might be right." He almost said "Kate." He'd have to get used to her wig and stop calling her by her name.

"I know it's early," Lev said, "but we'd be safer going to our separate rooms and staying there tonight. The less we move around the better. We have each other's room number. We can stay in touch on the room-to-room phone service."

"If there is anyone here who can finger us, I won't be recognized," Ethan said. "So, if you need anything from the gift shop, like a magazine or a paperback, let me know and I'll get it."

"Good idea, Ethan," Lev said. He glanced at Mel and Kate, and continued. "Under no conditions do I want either of you two wandering out of your respective rooms. It's only for one night, but the risk is too high."

Kate sighed. "Great having dinner with you, Dad. I'll say good night. See you all in the morning."

"I'll phone your rooms and let you know where to meet in the morning," Lev said.

Kate walked with Mel from the restaurant and waved at her Dad, a girlish smile on her face.

Chapter 51

After dinner with Jilly, Hank returned to his boat in the marina. His cell buzzed as he boarded.

"What?" He shouted. "When did you find this out?"

"Breaking news on TV," Jilly said. "Seems one of the security guards at the studio called a local TV station and reported that Kate had been held in a film vault for two days, then broke out and vanished."

"Do you know who it was?"

"No, the reporter said his source was anonymous."

"Yeah, and by morning every reporter working for those supermarket tabloids will be on her trail, along with dozens of paparazzi, their cameras loaded and their photo-fingers itching."

"What are we going to do, Hank?"

"Sit tight and hope my people locate her first. Don't talk to anybody. Understand?"

Jilly hung up and wondered nervously what Frank Primo would have done in a situation like this.

Jilly's problem worsened the next morning when she read the Los Angeles Times and discovered Kate was engaged to Melhi Pashagora, the son of Kumar Pashagora, owner of the largest film studio in India. Mr. Pashagora was offering a reward of one million dollars for the safe return of Kate Keenan to his business associates in Hollywood.

Jilly let the paper slip from her fingers. That son of a bitch Pashagora was going to get Kate, just as he said he would. By now there'd be hundreds of people searching for her.

And she was not the only person reading the same news.

Chapter 52

Ethan was up early and went down to get a newspaper. He glanced at the front page, rushed to his room and called Lev. "Call Kate and Mel to meet us in your room. And hurry."

Mel was the first to comment on the news: "We'll have dozens of people on our trail now. Dad's ransom offer will attract every bounty hunter in California. We should go to the cops now and save ourselves a lot of problems."

"If we do, Mel, the media will learn about Kate's computer program. Reporters can dig up more than you think." Ethan was speaking from experience. He'd had his problems with reporters years back when his agent had screwed his life up for him.

"We can't be on the run forever, Dad."

"We won't, Baby. Just long enough think of a way to solve this problem."

"Thanks to Joanie lending us her credit card, we won't leave an obvious paper trail," Lev said. "Mel, call room service and order breakfast for all of us. Then, I'm turning in the car. We'll rent a new one under Joanie's name."

Kate said, "Using Joanie's card?"

"Yeah, and I want you to wear your brown wig everywhere. It makes you look as ordinary as a mud puddle. Go with your Dad. Ethan can rent the car, showing his driver's license as ID. You'll be Joanie Malone. If they ask for your ID, say you can't drive, and give then the last four digits of your social security number. That sound okay, Ethan?"

"It should work. Dumping the Hollywood rental will slow them down. Tolomeo will have every rental agency in Hollywood checked and will have asked to be notified when and where the car gets turned back in," Lev said.

"Can he do that?" Kate asked.

"Put it this way, Kate: Tolomeo gets things to work by throwing money at whatever obstacles get in his way."

"Yeah, and of course, the Hollywood rumor mill will be in top gear. Vicky Vance, the Wicked Voice of the West will be having a field day," Ethan said.

"Brings back old memories, does it, Ethan?" Lev, asked softly. "That rumor mill is just as powerful now as it ever was." Lev snapped his fingers. "That's it. We'll use it to *our* advantage."

"Miss Information," said Ethan. "She's always a star."

"The town thrives on it, and the population of Hollywood notables and celebrities will eat it up. I learned a couple of hot items when Stacy Hart updated me at Forest Lawn before Primo's service."

Ethan turned at the mention of her name. "What did she

tell you?"

Room service delivered breakfast before Lev could answer. Once the waiter had left, Lev said, "Plenty." He grabbed a bagel, spread on some cream cheese and took a bite. "Jilly Suede is heir to Megastar studio, among other things."

Ethan poured himself another cup of coffee. "Toss that piece of info into Pattie Primo's lap and BOOM! The interest in our caper will fall off noticeably."

Lev grunted. "Vicky Vance's lap would make a better landing place."

"You're right, Lev. Pass the bagels."

The rental car return worked out fine. Ethan drove the new rental, followed by Kate driving Ethan's car containing Lev and Mel.

"Where the hell is Bullhead City?" Kate asked.

"About a hundred miles south of Las Vegas, across the Colorado River from Laughlin, Nevada," Lev muttered. "Just follow your dad. He knows the way."

A. G. Hayes

Chapter 53

Vicky Vance received a juicy tidbit from an anonymous caller saying Jilly Suede was heir to Frank Primo's Megastar studios. The caller quickly hung up. Vicky Vance was stunned. This morning's LA Times reported Kate had been a prisoner in a film vault on the Megastar lot before making her escape.

Vicky's forte was reporting rumors and innuendoes skillfully connecting them and dipping them in vats of doubt and fear. She knew her readers and their gluttony for simmered slices of scandal.

Vicky's long red fingernails clicked rapidly over her key board as she prepared her latest scoop.

Ethan pulled over a few miles outside Vegas and swapped cars with Lev. Kate wanted to ride with her father and visit awhile. Lev and Mel waited as Ethan pulled back onto the highway and they followed.

"Lev's thinking of renting a houseboat or something and making our way down river for a couple of days. He says it would be wise to stay off all major roads," Kate said.

Ethan blew out his cheeks. "You have a cell phone?"

"In my purse. Joanie loaned me one," Kate said as she

rummaged through her bag to find it.

"Good. Call Lev. I want to update him. By the way, be sure to turn off the GPS locator on the phone."

"Did that yesterday, Dad. But thanks for checking." She dialed and handed the phone over.

"Lev? It's me, Ethan. You flunked geography, right?" Before Lev could answer, Ethan said, "The river ride is out. We wouldn't get far enough downstream. You thought we could float back to California, right?"

Lev sounded unsure, "Yeah, well, close at least. Okay, Ethan, do you know any back roads into California?"

"Sure. How many do you need?"

Lev chuckled. "The quickest way with the least chance of anyone knowing we're back."

"Okay, but first we should grab a bite in Bullhead City. It's a long drive to California on the back roads. And make sure the GPS locator is turned off on your and Mel's phones."

Ethan handed the cell back to Kate; "Tell me more about this Tolomeo guy. He wasn't around when I was last in town."

It took twenty-five miles for Kate to bring her dad up to date.

"He sounds like a definite problem, and him being cozy with Jilly Suede adds another dimension to the trouble dynamic. When we stop to eat, make me a list of everyone involved so far."

They were on the outskirts of Bullhead City when Ethan pulled into the parking lot of a Kentucky Fried Chicken.

Minutes later, Kate was pushing a greasy piece of paper across the plastic tabletop and taking a final bite of a chicken leg.

"There you are, Dad, the list you asked for." Mel and Lev exchanged glances. Kate explained, "A different cast of characters since your days, but I bet not all that different in their methods of wheeling and dealing."

Ethan grunted, "William Shakespeare made the definitive statement in, *All About Nothing*."

Lev said quickly, "When you show up in Hollywood again, you may discover enemies you've forgotten about. Enemies waiting to finish you off."

Ethan wiped his fingers on an already tired napkin, "I never forget, Lev. Trust me. That's why I'm going to say it again. Don't phone Stacy like you promised. If you do, you'll be talking to those who want Kate's program and all us out of the way."

Lev frowned. "Stacy?"

"She's a publicist, and a good one. One of the best, in fact. I remember her from when I was a writer in Hollywood and my work was stolen and given to Don Ames."

"Stacy was part of that?"

"All I'm saying is, everybody in Hollywood is part of

something one way or another. The bigger they are, the more enmeshed they become in everything."

Chapter 54

The Burbank PD's search warrant for Megastar included the film vaults. The crime scene investigation was wrapping up when the two Feds who had investigated Vance's murder at Forest Lawn entered. Agent Harcourt looked as peevish as ever as he scanned the empty room. Agent Kirkland, at his side, wisecracked, "'Tales from the Crypt'."

Ignoring the remark, Harcourt turned to the CSI leader and asked, "Anything?"

"She was here, that's for sure. We've just finished doing the HDS."

Harcourt nodded, he knew HDS or high definition surveying involved reflecting a laser light off objects in the room and back to a digital sensor, creating three-dimensional spatial coordinates that are stored. He was thankful to be retiring soon; he was finding it hard to keep up with the new technology.

"Take a look in the back room next to the bathroom. Someone lost an arm." The rest of the CSI team grinned at Harcourt's reaction.

Rob's arm was in a thick plastic bag on the bench. A CSI policewoman was making notes.

"What is that?" Harcourt said pointing at the bag.

"Far as we can tell, Agent Harcourt, it's what's left of a robot." She pointed her pencil towards the desk. "We found the remains of an electro mechanical device, a robot I'd say. From what was left, it looks like it blew up and burned."

"A guy murdered in a choir loft and a robot in a film vault," Harcourt muttered.

"An *exploded* robot," added Kirkland.

"Yeah," said Harcourt. "This gal who escaped from here, she was a client of the guy we interviewed at Forest Lawn."

"Lev Leventhal. The publicist."

"You have his address?" Harcourt asked.

"I have a list of everyone we talked to."

"Good, let's go talk to him again."

Three hours later, Harcourt and Kirkland were re-interviewing Joanie Malone. "This is a murder investigation, Miz Malone. Every person in the church remains a suspect until the case is closed." Joanie had no answer for Harcourt when he asked why Lev hadn't been in for three days. "Everyone was instructed not to leave town without notifying Office of Homeland Security first."

"I never said he left town. I said he hasn't been in for three days."

"Is it usual for him not to show or call in?"

"No, it's not unusual. Sometimes he works from his home

office."

"But you phoned and got no answer, right? His client, Miz Keenan has been reported escaping from a film vault, and no one has heard from either of them for three days."

"I'm sure I'll hear from him," Joanie calmly insisted.

Harcourt straightened his skinny shoulders, "If he doesn't contact me in twenty-four hours, I'm putting out an all-points bulletin."

Joanie waited until the agents had left, then called the cell she'd loaned Kate.

A. G. Hayes

Chapter 55

Pattie Primo's morning was shattered when Vicky Vance phoned and brought her up to date on the pending loss of Charley Vee's due to a bad debt between her husband and Frank Primo. As heir to Frank Primo's studio, Jilly Suede was now the holder of the loan, a debt of one million five hundred thousand dollars.

Pattie screamed into her phone, "What are you talking about Vicky? The Will hasn't been read yet. You're a God-damn rumor monger! I'll sue for deformation of character."

"Calm down, Pattie. I'm your friend. You know that. I'm just giving you a heads up. We have to work together as always."

Pattie knew that was a crock, but settled down to hear more. "I'll talk to my lawyer, anyway. Someone is leaking information meant to harm me."

"Of course, you're right, Pattie. We have to discover who's behind all this, and why."

"We both know who's behind it: Hank Tolomeo! And it's due to that damn program of Kate's. I hope they never find that smart-ass little techy. This town would be far better off without her and that program!"

"She'll be back, mark my words. Kate Keenan is too big a prize for Tolomeo to let go. And when he does find her, he'll get her program and sell it to the highest bidder."

Pattie was sitting up in bed with the speakerphone on; lying beside her was Chaz Falconer, hair tousled, a crooked smile on his thin lips.

"Morning, Vicky dear," he drawled. "You left out the bit about Kumar Pashagora in Bollywood."

Vicky's tone changed. "What about him?"

"Just that his son, Melhi, plans to take Kate back to India and get married. Then Kumar will have legal possession of the program, and can run it and put Hollywood out of business. No one will be able to make movies as inexpensively as he will." Chaz paused, "One other little detail. In India, domicile is the key to matrimonial proceedings. Mumbai's High Court has held that Indian domicile is an essential condition for both the bride and groom. They both must reside in India at the time of their marriage ceremony. Kate will remain in India for the rest of her life."

Vicky was shocked at the news. "Who told you?"

"Kumar, when I signed a contract with him. I've been his American contact for quite a while now. Stella and I will remain here another couple of years or so, then move to India and live the high life."

"You're a jumped up little traitor Chaz. I'll see to it you

never work in this town again."

"Cool the rhetoric, Vicky. I read the book: Stella and I both have unbreakable seven-year contracts in Bollywood, so go ahead. We'll be paid whether Hollywood remembers us or not. And remember, you heard it here first."

The line went dead.

A. G. Hayes

Chapter 56

Across town, two stellar citizens of Hollywood were starting their day with coffee and doughnuts at International House of Pancakes. Ames and Villand hunched over a white plastic table discussing their new orders, received last night from Tolomeo.

Ames, haggard of face and suffering a nasty attack of diverticulitis, gazed dully at Villand and gently rubbed his painful left side. "Fuck Tolomeo. I've had it. Go here, do this, do that. I'm getting too old for this shit."

Villand took a third donut, licked his fingers and gulped down half a mug of coffee before saying, "Don, I feel your pain."

"Bullshit," replied Ames, and gave a halfhearted burp.

"I really do. Look. We do what he wants and it will be the last time. Trust me."

"Too bad you aren't a man of a thousand brains, Villand. I say Tolomeo will be the death of us."

"Don't talk like that, Don."

"I mean it. He called last night and told us to wire Leventhal's house for a remote controlled high explosive charge. Neither of us know jack shit about wiring or explosives."

"That's okay. We just go online and find out."

Ames looked even more pained. "That hit on the head has made you even crazier. Ever think perhaps he's setting us up? We agree, he waits until we're halfway through doing whatever you find out on line, he calls the cops and we're hauled off as suspected terrorists."

"I'd cop a plea and make a deal to give information on who stabbed Charles Vance in the choir loft."

"How do you know who killed Vance?"

"I know."

"Okay, Sherlock, who was it?"

"A skinny lady sitting in the back row of the church. She did the deed and was away before anyone had a clue Vance was dead."

"How do you know that?"

"Simple. I used one of my faces, a dab of lipstick and a dress. Tolomeo paid me ten big ones."

Ames's diverticular pain soared. "I'm not sitting here with a confessed murderer! I could go down for aiding and abetting. Forget about Leventhal's house." He shoved back his chair and rushed from the restaurant. Villand finished his donut, drained his cup and lit a cigarette. The tinsel of tinsel town was beginning to tarnish for many of the locals.

Chapter 57

Hank phoned from his yacht in the marina. "A rental company said the car Leventhal rented in Hollywood was turned in at one of their branches in Las Vegas. He paid the bill and left."

Jilly Suede's face was tight with worry. "Was Kate with him?"

"No."

"They could be anywhere. If she goes to the cops about us holding her prisoner on the lot…"

"She won't. Not yet, at least. I bet she'll contact that bank in Switzerland first, and approach another studio," Hank said.

"What about Mel?"

"Kumar has given him his orders. He's to take Kate to India along with her program and talk her into getting married over there, saying his father had finally given permission and welcomes her into the family."

"That bastard had everyone fooled, Hank. I had no idea he was working for his father."

"Blood's thicker than water, and Kate's program is thicker than blood to Kumar Pashagora."

Jilly fumed. "What about those two has-beens, Ames and

Villand? What about us?"

"I've made arrangements. Don't worry about us. But from here on out, we need to stick close together."

Not the most romantic suggestion in the world, Jilly thought, rolling her eyes upward, but Hank was usually right.

Chapter 58

Agents Harcourt and Kirkland saw red and blue flashing lights as they turned on to Lookout Mountain Avenue. An emergency vehicle sat parked at an angle outside Lev's house beside two black and whites.

The Medical Officer glanced up as they approached, and turned his flashlight beam on the body, "These fractures are from blunt force trauma, Agent Harcourt."

Harcourt leaned forward and studied the victim. "ID?"

The MO nodded and a police officer handed Harcourt a driver's license. Harcourt glanced at it, and indicated the house. "Anyone at home?"

The officer shook his head, "No one."

Harcourt didn't know the name on the driver's license, but Donald Ames was either leaving or going to visit someone in the house, and Harcourt guessed that someone was Lev Leventhal.

"We're going in, officer. Bust down the door."

A. G. Hayes

Chapter 59

Stace got a phone call as she entered her office. It was barely eight thirty in the morning, and the caller was Villand, who demanded an appointment with Stace at one. Villand said Tolomeo had insisted, saying it was of utmost importance. Stace begrudgingly agreed, then quickly dialed Vicky Vance.

"Vicky, it's vital that you phone me at exactly five after one. You do this and I'll have a big story for you, I promise. No, I can't tell you right now. Call me at exactly five after one and I'll tell you. Thanks, Vicky." Stacy hung up and stared at the instrument. It was now her lifeline.

She'd become involved with Hank Tolomeo over the last couple of years. The affair grew into a love/hate relationship, whereby Stace had been fool enough to slip information to Tolomeo on the inside workings of a number of Hollywood production companies. The knowledge she passed to him enhanced TolomeoTechnics' bottom line. Finally, she decided to end the affair. Tolomeo, however, threatened to break her by leaking controversial information, making her company seem as if it could not be trusted.

Stace had intentionally arrived early at the Forest Lawn

memorial for Charlie Vance on Tolomeo's orders. He was already waiting and suggested she stay until the end of the service. When asked why, he'd laughed, saying she would learn what would happen if she had any ideas about ending their working relationship. He left, returning later as if just arriving at the service.

Stace had almost told the whole story to Lev as they sat on the bench beneath the willow tree, waiting for the mourners to arrive.

Her morning at the office was been ruined by Villand's call. It was five minutes to one and Stace suddenly felt chilled. She reached for a sweater from the back of her chair.

"Your one o'clock is here, Ms. Hart," a voice announced from her desk intercom.

"Thank you, Sally. Send him in."

"It's a she, Ms. Hart, a Mrs. Applebaum."

"Oh," Stace paused. "Very well, Sally, send her in."

When the door opened, a small hunchbacked old woman entered and Stacy knew immediately she'd been right to call Vicky.

"Sit down, Franz. What do you want?"

"How did you recognize me, Stacy?" Franz Villand asked petulantly.

"You're getting too old. You've used up all your faces."

Villand sat down slowly; his eyes held a glint that frightened Stacy.

"I'm here as an emissary for Mr. Tolomeo, bitch. He wants you dead."

Stacy's eyes cut toward the phone wishing it to ring; it was almost five after one.

Villand reached inside his jacked and removed a long, thin-bladed knife. "Mr. Tolomeo wants it done quick and silent." He grasped the knife; his knuckles whitened. He smiled and began to push back the chair. Then the phone rang. Stace snatched it up.

"Vicky, Franz Villand is here in my office and he wants to talk to you." She turned toward Villand but he was already at the door.

He turned before exiting. "Very clever, Stacy. Next time, no appointment. You won't recognize who it is until the very last moment. Then it'll be too late."

Stace became aware of Vicky Vance's trumpeting voice and placed the phone to her ear. "You just saved my life, Vicky. Here's your scoop."

A. G. Hayes

Chapter 60

Ethan returned the rental in Bullhead City; they'd decided to use one car, Ethan's. It was after midnight. Ethan was at the wheel; Kate was half-asleep in the back seat, her head on Mel's shoulder. Bright moonlight reflected off the narrow ribbon of road unwinding ahead of them when her cell jangled.

"Hello."

"Kate?"

"Yes, who is this?"

"Joanie. Where are you?"

"Not sure, somewhere on a back road in California. You're lucky you got a signal. We're in the boonies. What's up?"

"I've been trying for hours. LAPD busted down Lev's front door at the house after finding Don Ames dead on the front porch. There's an All Points Bulletin out on him."

Lev turned from the front passenger seat. "Who is it?"

"It's Joanie. She's got some bad news." She passed the cell to Lev.

"Ames, dead on my front porch?" Lev said dazedly. "The cops kicked in my front door?"

"Agent Harcourt called me at home." Then she informed Lev about his office visit.

"So, I'm a suspect in Ames' death?"

"I'm sure everything will turn out fine, Lev. It's just a misunderstanding. By the way, I called your lawyer."

"Oh, thanks, Joanie. What else can you tell me?"

"Vicky Vance had a scoop about Primo leaving the studio to Jilly Suede and something about Charlie Vance owing a huge amount of money to Primo."

Lev sighed, "And?"

"You can imagine. Vicky and Pattie are at each other's throats."

Lev stared vacantly at the moonlit road and wondered if it was worth returning to Hollywood.

"Are you still there, Lev?"

"I'm afraid so."

"Good, Kate said the reception is spotty out there. When will you be back?"

"I don't know. I might turn myself in at Parker Center. I'll talk it over with Kate and then I'll call you back."

Ethan pulled over to the side of the deserted road and switched on the dome light: It was decision time.

Mel looked tense. His eyebrows drew together, giving his face a fierce look. His fingers tapped more rapidly on his knee.

Ethan leaned over the back of the driver's seat. "I'm not going to sit by and let Hollywood yank your chain like they did mine, Baby. Jilly Suede and Hank Tolomeo are going to answer for sticking you in that film vault and threatening you for your program. And don't give me anything about the media turning everything into a circus. From what I can see, it's already a five-ring circus with media stamped all over it." Ethan came on hard when roused.

"I know Dad, you're right. With what's happing with Lev and the cops, it might be best to turn ourselves in."

Mel cut in, "I prefer to contact the authorities and mediate a meeting where we can clear up any misunderstandings." His scowl, nervous fingers and agreement with the others made him seem overly concerned for their best welfare.

"Okay," said Lev. "Before or after we contact the Swiss bank?"

"Before, while we're all safely together. Who knows what'll happen once the police get involved," Kate said. "We'll need a secure environment to do the whole process."

Mel's face and hands relaxed, as if in relief, and he gave a quick grin.

Ethan started the engine. "Fine, then we have no need for back roads anymore. We just passed Amboy a few miles back. We'll stay on this road until we get to Ludlow, then pick up Highway Forty and head back to LA."

It was almost daylight when they arrived in Los Angeles. Lev recommended they go to his office, the safest place he could think of. Upon arrival, Lev suggested Kate get Mel and Ethan's password numbers and use Joanie's office phone to call the Swiss bank and download the program copying key. He removed Al Jolson from an inner pocket and passed it to Kate, saying he'd get the coffee started and be in his office when they were through.

Mel's eyes widened as if in surprise when he saw Lev had been carrying and hiding Al Jolson the whole time. His eyebrows narrowed once more.

Lev wearily slumped into his chair, dialed his lawyer and left a message that he was back in town, and then told Joanie's home machine that they were at the office. Done with the essential phone calls, he pondered: he'd been searching for Kate, now others were searching for them. Most importantly, they must stay out of Tolomeo's grip.

Kate concentrated on getting through to the Bezirbien-Uster Bank in Zurich. Finally, after a five minute wait on the line she received clearance to enter their combined 36-digit password.

During this time, Ethan nodded off in one of the armchairs in the waiting room. Mel slinked into the washroom, called Hank Tolomeo on his cell and updated him on their location. Tolomeo immediately gave Mel his orders, and then contacted Villand.

Mel returned and sat opposite Kate. "You get through okay?"

"Finally," she said, closing the lid of the laptop, "The program is fully functional for the next twenty-four hours." She began unpluging Al Jolson when suddenly Mel grabbed her arm.

"Leave it connected. I want to be sure everything works. Type in a few lines and create a picture for me."

"I'll need some of Lev's coffee. It smells so good."

"I'll get us both some. Just check everything out, okay?" Mel headed toward the aroma of coffee.

No longer wearing her drab wig, Kate's sumptuous red hair sparkled and she smiled as she typed. "The bride radiated happiness walking down the aisle, holding her father's arm and carrying a bouquet of dark blue violets."

Mel set a mug of steaming coffee beside her and leaned in to the screen. "Show me what you created."

Kate played back the short scene. Mel put his arms around her and whispered, "It will all come true, very soon now, my darling."

Joanie heard Lev's voice on her answering machine and tried to get to the phone before he hung up. She missed him by seconds. When she called back, the line was busy. She quickly dressed and started immediately for the office.

A. G. Hayes

Chapter 61

Kumar Pashagora, tired of the delays in getting Kate and her program to Mumbai, finally contacted associates in Los Angeles and ordered a special extraction team to bring Kate Keenan, Mel Pashagora, Frank Tolomeo and Jilly Suede to his office in Mumbai within 72 hours. Once located and brought together, they would be flown to Mexico and then on to London by private jet. Kate would be forced to marry Mel, and she, Frank and Jilly would remain in India until they died. He then ordered a hit team to assist the extraction team. He wanted no trail left. Once in Mumbai, India would be large enough to hide almost anything.

The hit team knew where their targets were thanks to a call placed by Frank Tolomeo to Kumar Pashagora, telling him that Mel had secretly phoned from Lev's office at 201 South La Cienega Boulevard. Tolomeo said he'd already arranged to send someone to clear up the problem and bring back Kate, the program and Mel. Unfortunately, Tolomeo, as the saying goes, had sent a boy to do a man's job.

Villand drove toward his target, hoping the car wouldn't stall at a light. He'd be able to buy more than just a new car with what Tolomeo was paying for this job. The Pashagora hit team, heading across town on the Hollywood freeway, drove a much nicer car.

Joanie parked in her usual place and switched off the engine. There was a strange car on the lot and she assumed it was the one Lev and the others had driven. She was about to get out, when a battered '96 Chevy limped into the car park. She recognized it at once as Villand's.

What happened next was like a bad dream. Joanie watched Villand get out of his car. Wearing a long drab raincoat, he stood beside the car, reached into an inside jacket pocket and removed a 9 millimeter automatic fitted with a suppressor. After inspecting it, he slid it into the right hand pocket of the raincoat.

Joanie scrunched down in her seat as Villand surveyed the lot. For a second she thought he might have seen her and was going to check her car. Thankfully, he didn't.

Keeping his right hand in his pocket, Villand walked slowly toward the building.

Joanie's hands shook as she punched the numbers into her cell phone: one, two, three anxious rings before Lev answered his cell.

"Lev! Get downstairs and lock the front door! Don't ask any questions, just do it now! Stay on the line, and then speak to me as soon as you have the door locked. Move!"

Lev wasted no time. Kate and Mel looked up as he

flashed past. Ethan was still asleep on the waiting room couch.

Lev went down the stairs three at a time and threw the dead bolt to the locked position.

"Okay, Joanie. The door's locked," he answered in between breaths. "What's going on?"

"Villand. He's outside heading to the entrance with a nine millimeter automatic. Get back upstairs and warn the others. I'm going to call 911. I'm under a blanket on the floor of my car outside the office. Bye."

A. G. Hayes

Chapter 62

Hank Tolomeo and Jilly Suede were sipping coffee in the main salon of Hank's 50-foot Aldon Flying Bridge Express twin diesel yacht.

"Sending that creep Villand to Lev Leventhal's office was a mistake. He's an old fool. Even if he does get in, he'll leave enough evidence behind to nail us."

"Thanks for the vote of confidence, Jilly." Hank got up from the table and looked out across the marina as the early morning fog began to swirl away in the first rays of sunshine. "Villand is going to lose face this morning, my dear. Successful or not, he'll be wiped out by Kumar's hit men."

Jilly looked unconvinced. "What do you mean?"

"When I called Kumar, he told me that his people will be bringing Kate, her program and Mel here to the yacht. We are to sail them to Mexico and rendezvous with a private jet that will fly us all to Chicago. We'll fly by a privately chartered commercial jet from Chicago to Mumbai by way of London."

Inwardly, Jilly was pleasantly surprised at Kumar's ability and cunning. Then again, the bastard had worked his way up from working in a small film studio to owning the largest movie enterprise in India.

"Can we trust him?" she asked.

"No, but for the moment, we'll have to. We've had too much bad publicity in this town. I've taken care of business at TolomeoTechnics. I sold out to a company that's been trying to buy me out for months. The transaction won't become public until long after we arrive in India. Also, my legal department has transferred all monies and other funds to a Mumbai banking concern."

Jilly's face clouded. "What about the possibility of extradition, Hank?"

"With my money and lawyers, it would take forever, if it ever happened at all." Tolomeo deeply regretted not getting Kate and her program out of the country and to Mumbai sooner. He would have if it hadn't been for Leventhal arranging for her to meet with Frank Primo.

Fast thinking and Jilly's organizing ability to outfit the film vault had bought them time to work on Kate. Then, just when success was in sight, the damn techy had escaped after destroying one of his robots.

"I don't like the idea of walking out on Frank's Will. It would have made me a rich woman."

"Listen to me, Jilly. Having one of your own security people call a TV news network and telling all, will not endear you to a jury when Pattie Primo contests the Will, which she will most certainly do. Don't even imagine she won't."

Jilly remained silent and thought fast. She'd been carrying out electronic transactions with her bank for years. What Hank was saying made sense: It was time to vanish. She picked up a phone. "Okay, Hank, what's the name of the bank in Mumbai? I'm going to make a transfer."

A. G. Hayes

Chapter 63

Villand heard someone behind the door and the lock click. For a moment, he was undecided whether to shoot off the lock. Then, with the weapon still gripped in his hand, he sidled around the outside of the building, looking for a back entrance. That was when the hit team saw him.

A dark haired woman in her mid-thirties pointed toward the building. "There he is, the creepy dude in the raincoat."

The driver, a swarthy man with curly hair and close-set eyes, grinned. "Roll down your window. I'll drive closer. Take him down fast." He started the engine and eased forward.

Villand looked back over his shoulder at the sound of the engine starting, and when he saw a car approaching, he panicked. Was it an unmarked police car?

He knew it wasn't the cops when he saw the elongated, silenced barrel of an automatic aimed at him. The soft phut-phut was inaudible as the woman planted two head shots into his final face—one of total astonishment.

"Now we'll take care of the others," the man said, parking the car. "This should be easy."

A. G. Hayes

Chapter 64

Upstairs, Lev assured them Joanie had called 911 and he had locked the front door.

Mel looked tense as Kate snuggled next to him and tightly held his hand.

"What about the back door, Lev?" Ethan asked, awakened by all the commotion.

"Bolted from the inside every night. It's the last thing we do before arming the alarm."

"Don't worry. I'll take care of you, Kate," Mel said softly. "Stay here while I take a peek outside." Mel rose and walked towards the window.

"Stay back from the window!" Lev yelled. "Everyone stay where you are away from the windows and just sit tight."

Mel bristled and shot Lev a vicious look as he slunk back to his seat.

The look was not lost on Lev. He'd noticed signs of a change in Mel in the last few hours. His eagerness to mediate with the authorities when they had returned to the office was one of them. He wondered if Mel had fooled him from day one, and had his own agenda as to why he wanted to find Kate.

Lev felt his cell phone vibrate; he'd switched off the ring tone after speaking to Joanie.

"Villand was just shot dead by two people in a car," Joanie said huskily. "They drove on to the parking lot after I called you. I came up from under the blanket when I heard their car. I thought it was the cops."

"Are you okay?"

"I'm fine, but the police aren't here yet. The couple in the car are trying to find a way into the building."

"Don't let them see you, Joanie."

"Roger that. Should I make a dash and get off the lot?"

"No. Stay put until the police get there."

The two-story building containing Lev's office dated back to the early thirties. Part brick and part stucco, it was originally built for storage. The top floor was later redesigned as office space. The entire ground floor was a satellite book depository for a publishing house back east. The only entrances to the second floor were front and back, and both were secure.

A loud crash and a shower of glass across the floor announced the arrival of a tear gas grenade. Lev moved with amazing agility, grabbing his metal wastebasket, scooping up the smoking canister, and hurling the basket out the window leaving only a trace of acrid, eye-burning odor in the room.

"Ethan!" Lev yelled. "Go into the bathroom and wet

down anything you see to put over our mouths and breathe through. Whoever's out there is serious."

Ethan moved fast, but Mel moved faster. It was likely this was the hit team sent to get him, Kate, the computer and now Al Jolson out of the office and down to the marina. It had to be. Time was running out.

While Ethan returned with wet washcloths and towels, Mel took the opportunity to grab a stiletto-like letter opener off Joanie's desk and secrete it up the sleeve of his jacket. Lev, fearing a second tear gas canister, ordered everyone into the small windowless kitchenette.

As Kate got to her feet, she tucked Al Jolson into her computer bag, slung the computer and device around her shoulder and started for the kitchenette. That was the move Mel needed.

"We'll be less susceptible to the tear gas if…" Lev's voice faded when he saw Mel holding Kate in one hand, the other gripping a letter opener, the sharp point pressed against Kate's jugular.

"You two get in the kitchenette. Kate and I are leaving," Mel hissed. Ethan made a move toward him. "Back off, Ethan, you don't want to be responsible for Kate's death, do you? Get in there. I mean it."

"Stay back, Dad," Kate pleaded. "Please. He means what he says."

"She goes with me and no harm will come to her." With his arm around her shoulders and the letter opener still held against her neck, they backed out of the room and down the stairs. In seconds, he had the door front door unlocked and was out in the parking lot.

The curly haired man saw them first. "There they are! C'mon!" Tossing aside the tear-gas launcher, he and the dark haired killer ran to their car and drove toward Kate and Mel. The woman opened the back passenger door, yelling for them to get in.

Mel pushed Kate in first, followed and slammed the door shut. The car burned rubber heading across the lot and out onto La Cienega Boulevard.

Within seconds of the car leaving, Lev and Ethan were in the parking lot. The car was gone.

A double beep-beep issued from Joanie's car. As they ran toward it, she swung open the doors.

"Get in. I saw them leave. They headed south."

Lev sat next to her, Ethan in the back seat. "I can't believe all this has happened and no one's showed up to help us," Lev gasped. "You called 911, right?"

"I did," Joanie replied as she sped across the lot and turned south. In the distance, police sirens sounded. Lev and Joanie exchanged glances.

"We must catch that car," Lev urged.

Ahead, La Cienega Boulevard was almost empty of traffic, unusual for this early hour of the morning. There was no sign of their quarry.

"They've vanished. Now we have no idea where they are," Joanie wailed.

"Keep driving," Lev muttered. "They're probably ahead somewhere."

Ethan leaned across the front seat, "Sorry I bad-mouthed Stacy Hart. If I'd let you stay in touch with Stace on a daily basis, this might never have happened."

Lev twisted in his seat. "What do you mean?"

"It's a long story. Let's say it'd be a good idea if you give her a call, and see what she knows. Blame me for not calling each day as you promised."

"Nothing!" Joanie cursed when the car they were seeking never showed up.

"Okay. Joanie, then let's get back to the office. I'll tell the cops what we know, and then call Stace."

A. G. Hayes

Chapter 65

Joanie turned onto the office parking lot. A yellow police tape fluttered across the entrance and an LAPD officer stopped them.

"Now they show up," Lev growled, rolling down his window. "Officer, inform whoever is in charge that we were in the building when it was attacked. My name is Lev Leventhal."

The uniform walked over to a group of suits and pointed toward their car. He returned, lifted the tape and jerked his thumb—drive in.

The skinny figure of Agent Harcourt stood next to a body bag. He looked up said something to a plain-clothed cop and stalked over to them. From his look, it was apparent they were not welcome.

Harcourt leaned through the open car window. "*You,* Mr. Leventhal, were told not to leave town."

"It was a matter of life and death," Lev replied.

"We'll see about that. What's this about being attacked in the building? We got a call someone was shot."

"Right, and someone fired a tear gas canister through the window. I threw it back out before it overcame us."

"Yeah, we found it," Harcourt growled.

"Plus one of my clients was abducted with a letter opener held to her throat."

Harcourt shook his head in disbelief and jerked his thumb over his shoulder, "Get out of the car; the three of you are going to Westwood."

"Hey, hold it mister. His client," Ethan pointed at Lev, "is my daughter. We lit out after her and the bad guys, but they got away. What are you people going to do about that?" While Ethan offered his challenge, Joanie made a fast call to Lev's lawyer before they were transferred to a black and white.

At the Federal building in Westwood, Lev explained the situation, from the wrap party to the moment when Mel took Kate hostage. Lev's lawyer, now also present, added his assurance that from now on, Lev would not leave town and that they would notify Harcourt of any new developments.

Harcourt silently recorded every word. Finished, he said, "The time is eleven fifteen a.m. and the Leventhal interview is ended." Switching off the machine, he tilted back his chair. "I'm going to give you some information Leventhal, then maybe you'll pay more attention. The Office of Homeland Security was on this case from the moment Frank Primo died at the wrap party." Lev opened his mouth to speak, but Harcourt shook his head and continued. "Burbank, Glendale, and

Los Angeles Police Departments have also become involved. Agent Kirkland and I have been tied at the hip to all three."

A plainclothesman leaned in, "OHS, working in concert with The National Security Agency, NSA, intends to resolve what could turn out to be a serious loss to America's future security." The man nodded at Harcourt.

"Thanks, captain." Harcourt continued addressing the trio: "The program Miz Keenan designed is of interest to the NSA. The possibilities of its utilization in military circles are beyond imagination. OHS is fully aware that a Mister Kumar Pashagora in Mumbai has been, and still is supplying aid and information to radical Muslim factions in Pakistan, hoping to destabilize the region."

The hair on the back of Lev's neck rose.

"On the surface, Kumar Pashagora appears to be exactly what he is: a wealthy India film industry magnate, well known and respected in the field of entertainment worldwide. With such credentials, he is able to wield considerable power. OHS can't simply reach into India and arrest him, but we definitely intend to stop him from getting the young girl and her computer program."

"That's what *we've* been doing, Agent Harcourt!" Lev exclaimed.

Harcourt smiled thinly. "Yes, we know, and we want you to continue. They know you're looking for Kate, so any sudden change in tactics might alert them about us."

"Fox and Hounds," Lev's mind raced back to Kate's reference to NSA offering her a position after graduation. Her mention of feeling followed and the car tailing Mel from the parking lot to his apartment suddenly made sense.

"You could say that, Mr. Leventhal, but remember: OHS is the Master of the Hounds. Continue to go about your task. We'll be close by and ready when needed." Harcourt scribbled on a piece of paper and handed it to Lev. "My cell number. Call anytime, day or night."

On the cab ride back to Lev's office, Ethan suggested it was time to call Stace. Lev agreed.

Chapter 66

"Lev, where are you? You were supposed to call every day and keep me posted!" Stacy Hart was pissed.

"It's a long story, Stace. You'll understand when I explain everything."

"Listen to me Lev. Pattie Primo called with Vicky Vance screaming and yelling on her speakerphone. Chaz Falconer was with her and cut in with that nonchalant drawl of his and said Mel was in on everything from the beginning. Mel Pashagora intends to shanghai Kate to India and marry her. Once they are married in the eyes of Indian law, Pashagora will see to it Kate and her program remain in Pashagora possession. That means she'll be a prisoner there the rest of her life.

"Then Falconer boasted that he and Stella Rae had served as the American contacts for Kumar Pashagora, and when the right time came, they'd head off to India, where they planned to live high and continue working with Kumar. If you'd called me every day you would have known this two days ago."

"You're right, Stace. I've just got back from the Federal Building in Westwood and received a similar lecture." Lev made no mention of Harcourt's Fox and Hounds operation.

He retold Stacy about their trip from the moment they'd left town after she had dropped him off in Hollywood at the car rental agency, right up to Mel taking Kate by force from the office to a car waiting outside. He added that no one, including the Feds, knew where Kate and Mel were.

"That's a lot of drama, Lev." Stacy said quietly. "When can we meet?

"It's noon now. How about in an hour in your office? I have someone for you to meet."

"Who's that?"

"It's a part of a long story, Stace."

"Okay, one o'clock here at my office." Stace's reluctance to hang up revealed her craving to hear the rest of the story.

At one o'clock precisely, Stace heard a light knock on the door. She glanced up from her desk to see Lev and Ethan enter. She leaned back in her chair and indicated Ethan. "Is he part of the long story?"

Ethan answered, "Guess I am, Stace."

"Sit down both of you. Where did you spring from Ethan? It's been a while since we last met," Stace said.

"Arizona, and I'd still be there if Kate hadn't called me," Ethan said.

"Kate?"

"Yeah, and it's my fault that Lev didn't stay in touch like he promised. After being screwed over by my crooked agent and the breakup with Kate's mom, you were the only person in this town who tried to help me. I ignored your help, became a full time drunk and took off to Arizona. I've been living in a trailer park for almost two years," Ethan admitted. He rubbed his forehead slowly, "A lonely existence: sun, fresh air, and my only friend a dog who loves bacon rinds. I finally got tired of feeling sorry for myself, quit the booze and started to write again. Then I got a message from Kate."

"You should put it all in your book, Ethan," Stace replied.

"Already have, Stace, and you're in it, too."

Lev broke the trance between them by asking if she knew whether Tolomeo was in town.

"I heard he's aboard his yacht, the *Technocrat*, in Marina Del Rey. Jilly's with him." She paused. "You think Mel might take Kate to the yacht?"

"It's a possibility Ethan and I intend to explore. Do you know where he keeps his yacht in the marina? The dock, the slip or whatever they're called?" Lev asked.

"I've been on board the *Technocrat* a couple of times. I don't know the actual address but I'm certain I could lead you to it," Stace offered, inviting herself.

A. G. Hayes

Chapter 67

"What if we didn't sail to Mexico, Hank? What if we leave the boat, hide out somewhere, and keep the program?"

Hank stared at Jilly. "Are you crazy? Do you have a death wish or something, because our deaths are what would result if we tried to thwart Kumar Pashagora."

Jilly pouted. "I suppose you're right."

"Suppose? I can't imagine how Frank Primo could entrust you to help run his studio. You're nuts, Jilly."

"Maybe I don't want to live in India."

"You try a stunt like you just proposed and you won't get to stay alive anywhere. We're going through with his plan and will deliver to him Kate and the program. Once we've done that, he won't care what we do."

"You ever think that by now someone will have figured out where Kumar's thugs will take Kate?" Jilly asked.

"Yeah, and as soon as Mel and Kate get here, we move out."

Jilly brightened, "Where to?"

"I've arranged to have the yacht go into dry dock for its yearly maintenance. It'll be out of the water for a week. After Kumar's people deliver Kate and Mel and we've left my yacht

in the dry dock, we'll go board a charter vessel I have waiting, and head for Mexico."

Jilly glanced out the cabin window. A car had stopped and
Mel got out, gripping Kate's arm. "They're here."

"Fine, after they come aboard and the car leaves, we
move out."

"Kumar's people, that curly haired man and mean-looking
woman, will drop them off and leave, just like that?"

"Yes, but they'll never make it back to LA."

Her face tightened, "Meaning?"

Hank watched the car pull away, "Arrangements, Jilly.
Kumar leaves nothing to chance."

Kate struggled against Mel as he pulled her aboard.
Within minutes, Hank had moved the yacht out of the slip
into the channel.

"You'll never get away with this Mel! Kidnapping is a
Federal offense," Kate grated.

"True, but only if we're caught," Mel shot back.

"You will be, I'm sure of it. Once Lev finds Hank's yacht
is missing, the coast guard will find and will haul this yacht
back."

"The Coast Guard won't know where we are. If they
bother go to the trouble of locating this yacht, they'll find it in
a dry dock facility. Hank's arranged for us to switch to a charter Grand Banks Forty-two that'll be waiting to sail us down

to Ensenada, Mexico, where we'll be picked up and driven to a private airstrip to begin the next step on our journey to India," Jilly informed her.

Kate slumped in her seat at the galley table, knowing that if no one rescued her, she knew she would harassed until she relinquished her program to the Pashagoras.

Jilly Suede leaned across the galley table and narrowed her eyes. "Listen, girl. Just thank you're lucky stars you weren't killed and your program taken the night your ass was hauled to the film vault. If I'd have had my way, that's what would have happened."

"So, who stopped you?"

Jilly jerked her thumb toward Mel. "He did. He told us that your computer program was useless without the password." Kate flashed back to the unbelievable moment when Mel had dragged her from Lev's office with the tip of a letter opener pressed against her neck.

The curly haired hit man checked his side mirror, successfully making the transition from the Marina to the Santa Monica Freeway. All clear, he stepped up his speed to merge with traffic on the 405. Three seconds later, their car exploded in a ball of flame, slid across three lanes, smashed into the center divider and crumpled into a twisted smoking tangle of metal.

A. G. Hayes

Chapter 68

"I could have sworn this was the right place." Stacy Hart muttered as she walked back and forth on the sidewalk looking down at an empty slip. Already dusk, it was becoming increasingly difficult to distinguish one yacht from another.

"We could knock on hatches and ask someone," Ethan suggested, indicating the other boats in the dock.

"We need a key to get onto the dock," Lev said.

"Wait! I just saw someone on that boat." Stace pointed to a sailboat, sails fluttering in the night breeze. "I'll call and attract their attention."

"I'll call," Ethan countermanded, cupping his hands and bellowed, "Ahoy, sailboat!"

"The name on the stern is Sca Dwarf. Try calling Sea Dwarf." Lev suggested.

Ethan did, and this time a man came up on deck. "We're looking for Hank Tolomeo. This is his slip isn't it?"

"Yeah, but you missed him. His yacht left about ten minutes ago."

"Was Hank onboard?"

"He was earlier. I was busy below, and just caught a glimpse of the hull through a porthole as the yacht moved out. Can't say with certainty that I saw him at the helm."

"Okay, thanks," Ethan shouted. "Well, you had the right slip, Stace. We just didn't get here soon enough."

"Can't we notify the Coast Guard and ask them to pull him over?"

"For what, Stace? We don't know for certain Kate's even on the yacht."

"There must be a way to find out. Call agent Harcourt and tell him we think she's being shanghaied."

Despite the situation, Lev had to smile. "I bet it would be the first time Harcourt ever got a call like that."

Nonetheless, Lev called and brought Harcourt up to date.

"You're on Los Angeles Sheriff's Department turf, so now I'll have to tie in with a fourth law enforcement agency. They're going to love you, Leventhal."

Lev added the information on Chaz and Stella, closed his cell, slipped it into his pocket and stared into the watery darkness. If Kate was on the yacht, she could be miles away already.

Kumar Pashagora had the rich man's ability of eliminating any 'loose strands' that stood in the way of in his international skullduggery, and there were two left to go: Chaz and Stella.

Chapter 69

The thud and clash of drums and cymbals beneath the dissonant wails of electronic guitars shook the drapes causing the amplified sounds to ricochet around Stella Rae's living room.

Stella, slumped on a once exquisite Victorian settee, now stained with red wine, cigarette burns and other unnamed blotches, stared with a glazed look out of the window holding a glass of vodka. It was three in the afternoon.

"Stella," Chaz shouted as he entered. "Hey, come alive, we have an emergency. Kumar called."

"Fuck off," she shouted, taking another deep suck from her glass. "I'm through with Pashagora calling the tune."

"We're to join Hank at the dry dock in Seal Beach, and go with them to Mexico and on to India. He's ordered us out of here, Stella. A million tax free dollars and life in an exotic land."

She nodded but remained silent.

"Put the glass down and listen up, you dumb bitch."

The heavy cut crystal glass barely missed Chaz's left ear before smashing into pieces against the wall.

He sighed, walked across the room and slapped her hard

across the face. "Fine, if that's the way you want it, then I'll take care of myself and you can stay here." Chaz reached across and picked up the almost empty vodka bottle from the coffee table. "Here, finish it off. There's more in the kitchen if you can walk that far."

The slap had knocked a little sense into her dulled mind. If he left her, Stella knew she'd be dead in a week, and by her own hand, not Pashagora's. "You can't just walk out and leave me," she slurred.

"Oh, yes, I can. Vicky Vance is about to feature us in her gossip column and we'll be thrown out of town. I'm not about to wait for that to happen."

"You screwed up telling her anything in the first place, Chaz, and you know it." She took a pull from the bottle.

"You're right. It was dumb. But not as stupid as sticking around and letting Vance tie us in with Jilly and Tolomeo."

Stella tipped the bottle upside down and watched the last drops drip onto the thick pile carpet. She started to speak then her eyes rolled back in her head and she crumpled into the couch, out cold.

Chaz kicked the empty bottle aside and left the room. He'd carry out Kumar's orders and leave. Stella'd made her own choice.

Chapter 70

Since 9/11, America had gradually become accustomed to an undercurrent of intrigue in all walks of everyday life and possibly unknowingly, come to accepted it. Thus, the rights of individuals, no matter whom, helped cover the subterfuge of others. By constant manipulation of greedy and fame-crazed personalities, Kumar Pashagora was able to move in on Hollywood's exclusive networking system.

Vicky Vance's gossip irritated Kumar, and such loose strands infuriated him. He told himself repeatedly that the tittle-tattle would, like all other celebrity stories, fade with time. In the end, he would permit her to live, as she would be easy to control now. However, he didn't intend to leave any-one else alive with knowledge of his plans, and Kate, the program and Mel would remain forever in Mumbai.

A. G. Hayes

Chapter 71

The month of March in Southern California can be sunny, dry, wet or cold. This time around, it was wet. Rainwater gushed from broken gutters of a derelict old building that had once been the packinghouse headquarters of Pacific Fruits from the Sea.'

Sitting on four acres of land located between Long and Seal Beaches, the structure, long abandoned, had been crumbling around the edges for decades. Kumar Pashagora had purchased the parcel years ago, and now the acreage alone was worth triple what he'd paid.

A shadowy figure inside a dome-tent erected in a corner of the dilapidated factory watched a video image transmitted from a security camera a thousand feet away.

Several hours would pass before Tolomeo's yacht arrived at the nearby dry dock and Scumbag, Kate's guard from the film vault, would see a clear picture of the yacht when she arrived at dawn's early light.

A. G. Hayes

Chapter 72

When Stella awoke, it was dark outside. Her housekeeper had covered her with a blanket and left. She was alone and scared. Her head thumped and her hands shook as she reached for the phone.

Vicky Vance answered. "Hello, is that you Stella? Are you all right?"

"No, I'm not. I must talk to you."

"Go ahead, dear, I'm all ears."

"No. In person, Vicky. Not on the phone. What I have to tell you is not for phone chat." Stella's voice was shaky.

"Do you want to come over now, Stella?"

"No way, I'm hung over and don't want to drive."

Vicky, smelling a story, replied quickly, "Stay still, be calm, and make coffee. I'm on my way."

Stella showered and drank three cups of coffee, but she remained shaky. Headlights shone up the driveway and Stella went to the front door to greet her as Vicky slammed the car door shut and headed up the steps.

A few days earlier, as Lev and Mel were leaving the Wake at Musso and Frank's, Lev mentioned that Vicky and Charles Vance were not very close as man and wife; he'd been right.

Vicky eye's narrowed with concern as Stella poured out her story of how Chaz had become involved in Kumar Pashagora's intrigues and dragged her reluctantly into the web.

"You did the right thing to call me, Stella. This is awful."

"Chaz has gone to join Hank and the others. I could be charged with aiding and abetting a terrorist."

"Now, just a minute, Stella. I wouldn't go so far as to call Pashagora a terrorist. An overzealous business man, maybe, but not a terrorist."

"Chaz wouldn't agree. He told me that once in India, the program would be adapted for military use. That's why he left in a hurry while he had the chance. What can I do?" she sobbed.

"For now, stay at home. I'll take care of everything. When your housekeeper comes tomorrow, tell her you're not well and stay in the house. Don't make any phone calls and don't answer the phone, okay? I'll come by tomorrow." If her vision hadn't been blurred, Stella might have seen Vicky's smile at her plan to keep Stella isolated and beholden only to Vicky.

"Thank you, Vicky. Thank God, There's someone in this town I can trust."

"It's all right, dear. We ladies have to stick together, I always say. Now turn in, and try to get some sleep."

Stella saw her to the door and walked back to her living

room. Before Vicky had driven out of the driveway, went to kitchen and opened a fresh bottle of vodka.

A. G. Hayes

Chapter 73

Joanie had overseen the window repair at the office and cleaned the place. Several hours later, after making fresh coffee, she sat at her desk and dialed Lev's number.

"Where are you Lev?"

"Joanie, I was just about to call you. We're down at the marina. Ethan and Stace are with me and we're heading to the Sheriff's office. We think Kate's been kidnapped by Hank. Listen, gotta go. I'll call you soon. I promise."

Lev parked in the lot at the Sheriff's office on Fiji Way. "Let's go inside and introduce ourselves before Harcourt arrives."

The desk sergeant informed Lev that Agent Harcourt had already called and talked with the captain on duty, and she was ready to see them.

Captain Patricia Powers, a well-built woman of color around forty with a touch of gray in her hair, looked up from her paper work when the sergeant knocked on her door and entered, saying, "Mr. Leventhal and party, Ma'am."

"Ah, yes," she replied. "Come in, Mr. Leventhal. Sit down." She indicated a couch and chair. Lev took the chair and introduced Stace and Ethan who shared the couch.

"I hear you've been alerted to the problem at hand and will bring us up to date," Lev said.

Captain Powers' face clouded. "Yes, that's correct. And we've alerted the Coast Guard and radio contact has been made with other marinas to be on the lookout for a fifty-foot Aldon Flyingbridge Express, especially marinas and docks with a dry dock facility. Agent Harcourt has gone ahead to the Long Beach area as he feels that could be the yacht's most likely destination." The captain smiled with satisfaction at having all the available information at her fingertips, her eyes twinkling at Lev's surprise. "One of agent Harcourt's men questioned someone in a slip next to where the yacht is nor-mally docked, and was informed the yacht was going in for its annual dry dock service," she explained.

"We also talked to a man on a sail boat. He said the yacht had left, but nothing about a dry dock," Lev informed.

"Perhaps you didn't ask the right questions, or you left too soon," the captain chided.

She, of course, was right. Lev wondered how Harcourt had someone there so quickly, and then remembered Har-court's remark about Fox and Hounds and OHS being the Master of the Hounds. "Did agent Harcourt say where exactly in the Long Beach area?" Lev asked, leaning forward eagerly.

Powers shook her head, "No."

"Long Beach covers a large area, Captain," Ethan remarked.

"It does. However, as I mentioned, we've alerted the Coast Guard and sent radio alerts to all the marinas to be on the lookout for the yacht just in case they change their minds."

Stace asked, "If the craft heads for a dry dock as everyone suspects, what would Hank use as transport? If he does have Kate, he'll have to keep moving."

"He could have a car or truck waiting," Ethan suggested.

"Yeah," Lev nodded. "Being at the docks, he could also have a boat waiting. Kate said they planned to take her to India. To avoid all OHS contact, a clever man like Tolomeo might switch boats, cruise to Mexico and begin the flight to Mumbai from there."

"If he does that, Lev, no one will have a description of the boat or much of a chance of finding them."

The storm that battered the old warehouse near Seal Beach moved northward, and rain began slanting hard across Marina Del Rey.

"Wherever the yacht is, this weather's going to slow her down some," Captain Powers said, glancing at her office window as a gust of wind rattled the frame, and pressed her intercom button. "Sam, print out a list of all dry docks in and around Long and Seal Beaches and bring them here." She looked directly at Ethan. "I'm sure agent Harcourt has a list, and I've no doubt you intend to go down there and poke around. I would, too, if I had a daughter in the same predicament. I thought this list might be helpful."

"Thank you, Ma'am, we appreciate that," Ethan remarked.

"We all do," added Lev. "Thanks again."

Chapter 74

Joanie was about to leave the office when the phone rang. She returned to her desk and scooped it up. "Hello?"

It was Stella Rae. "Let me talk with Lev, it's very important."

Joanie caught the slur in her voice and told her Lev was not in the office.

"Shit! It's a matter of life and death, and I mean it! Can you give me a number where I can reach him?"

With all that was going on, Joanie didn't hesitate.

Rain falling heavily outside the Sheriff's office. Lev's windshield wipers were slashing on high speed with only minimal effect, when his cell vibrated. "Reach into my right jacket pocket, Stace, and answer my cell."

"Hello, who is this? Yes, he's here. He's driving in a rain storm and wants me to convey your message. Speak louder, I can hardly hear you. Who? Stella Rae? What do you want at this time of the night, Stella?" Laying the phone on the carseat between them, Stacy said, "She'll only talk directly to you."

Lev nodded, "The Western Avenue off ramp is coming up. Tell her I'll pull off there and we can talk."

Lev pulled to a stop on Western. "Go ahead Stella, what is it?"

Stella told him Chaz had walked out on her, and was going to join Hank and the others.

"You mean you know where Hank's taking his boat?"

"Yes, and I have a bad feeling about it. Do you have a map, Lev?"

"Sure, hold on." Rummaging in the glove compartment, he pulled out a battered Southern California map book. "Okay, Stella, tell me." Stace grabbed a notebook and pen from her purse and snapped on the dome light.

Lev repeated aloud each direction Stella gave. "Get back onto the four-oh-five and head east toward Seal Beach. Take the Lakewood off-ramp and stay on Lakewood Boulevard south all the way to Second Street."

Stace wrote each repeated word.

"Turn left onto Second Street. It dead-ends at an old unused warehouse complex. We probably won't see the building in the dark. It's in the middle of about four acres of empty land, located near the turning-basin in the Seal Beach marina."

"Lev," Stella implored. "Hank Tolomeo should arrive there early in the morning. He plans to secretly switch to a waiting charter boat. I was down there with Chaz on an errand for Pashagora about two months ago. It's a rough area.

And Lev, be careful. Pashagora has the warehouse and surrounding wasteland covered with concealed high-tech video security cameras. You'll be seen, rain or not."

"Thanks, Stella. You okay?"

"No, Lev, not really. Good luck." Lev's phone clicked off. The driver of a black Ford Explorer parked in the shadows five hundred yards behind Lev watched the dome light go out, headlights come on and the car make a U-turn north heading back to I-405.

"He's moving, sir."

"Fine, keep me updated," Harcourt said. "We're on our way."

A. G. Hayes

Chapter 75

Chaz Falconer had taken his time after leaving Stella at the house. He'd stopped for dinner, then completed the drive to the Seal Beach rendezvous. Now, as he approached the wasteland surrounding the warehouse, he carried a flashlight, aimed it toward the derelict building and pressed the switch three times. Seconds later, three quick winks of light issued from the building. Contact made.

Five minutes before, Lev had stopped at the end Second Street. A lone street lamp shone dimly through a swirling halo of rain.

"What a dismal place," he remarked as he turned off the engine.

"Can you see the warehouse?" Stace asked, wiping the steamy car windows with a Kleenex. "And don't forget what Stella said about the security cameras being able to see us."

"That's why I drove the last quarter mile with the lights off, Stace." He pointed at the distant street light. "That was my beacon. Ethan, reach up and turn off the switch on the dome light before I open a door."

"Okay, it's off."

"Good, stay here until I get back."

"Hold it, Lev," Ethan said quickly. "We go together. Stace can wait here. Either of you have a problem with that?"

Stace unclasped her white-knuckled hands, relieved to stay in the car.

"Lock the doors after we leave," Lev ordered. "The keys are in the ignition. If anything goes wrong, call Harcourt and get the hell out of this area."

"What's a turning basin?" Ethan whispered as they picked their way down the side of the waste ground.

"A place where a boat can turn around at the end of a dead end channel," Lev suddenly reached out and grabbed Ethan's arm. "Hold it. Stay still." They both froze.

"What is it?" Ethan whispered.

"Over there on your right, in the middle distance, a flicker of light." Ethan squinted into the driving rain.

"There! Did you see it?" Lev said.

"Yeah, looked like a flashlight, just a quick glimmer."

"Okay, let's get back to the car. This is a 'No Man's Land' and we're not going to try to cross it."

Stace, alone in the car felt a shiver of fear run through her veins. Her years of intrigue and pressure of running a high-powered publicity office in Hollywood had, over the last few days, began to tell on her. She had become, unknowingly at first, a part of what was unfolding out there in the darkness. She knew Tolomeo and Kumar Pashagora had used her, along with other fools.

Groping their way back to the car had taken almost five minutes. Lev rapped on the driver's side window, "Stace, open up it's us." Nothing happened. Lev cupped his hands and peered through steamy window then rapped hard, "Hey, Stace, open up." He tugged the door handle; it wouldn't open. Ethan went around to the passenger side and checked the doors. It was no use, Stace didn't answer and all the doors were locked.

A. G. Hayes

Chapter 76

It happened swiftly. The driver's door flew open and Stace was hauled out of the vehicle. Now, slumped next to Harcourt in the back seat of an agency car, she realized who it was beside her.

"Sorry, Miz Hart. We had to move fast. I assure you, your life was in jeopardy."

Stace blurted. "But I had the doors locked!"

"We, like our adversaries, have means of overcoming locked doors."

"What happened to Lev and Ethan?"

"They're okay. Two of my men have them. We'll meet at the Harbormaster's office."

A. G. Hayes

Chapter 77

Scumbag focused a security camera across the acreage through the rain and mist, and held a zoom image on two men exiting a car.

"Take a look, Chaz."

Chaz moved in close. "Damn, that's a hell of a sharp image, despite this shitty weather."

"Yeah, TolomeoTechnics makes cutting edge thermals. The heat from the car's engine acted like a magnet soon as I switched this camera on."

"How come we didn't see them sooner?"

"I can't monitor every camera at once. I've been scoping out the marina and the channel. I just now turned this baby on. Hey! Check this out, there's another couple of guys in the picture."

"They look like cops," Chaz muttered.

Scumbag kept the camera on the men and zoomed in tighter. "You recognize any of the four?"

"Yeah, one of them looks like Lev Leventhal. He's that meddling theatrical agent who thinks he's a detective."

"If it's Leventhal, someone's been mouthing off too much. Tolomeo ain't going to like this."

"What do you mean?"

"The plan is for Tolomeo to sail up the channel, dock in the marina then switch to a waiting charter boat that'll take them Mexico."

"I know that. I'm supposed to join them and go to Mexico, too."

"Man, you're all screwed up," Scumbag sneered. "You and me are here to be certain Jilly Suede never leaves alive."

"Jilly?"

"Yeah, someone wants to get rid of her, and I can't blame them."

"But Hank said I was going with them!" Chaz yelled.

"Hold it down, man, and listen to me: You and me are here to take care of Jilly. To see she never leaves this place after we bring her here from the yacht."

"I'm not going to be part of a murder. No way. I'm getting out of here."

As Chaz turned to leave, Scumbag grabbed him by the collar and yanked him back. "Fine, then I'll have to kill you first and then do Jilly. No problem."

The impact of what Scumbag was saying finally soaked in. Chaz had to run. Now. But Scumbag was armed and he wasn't.

Chapter 78

Halyards snapping against aluminum masts of a forest of sailboats bobbing in their slips beat a steady tattoo as the storm moved north. Only one or two lights dotted the darkness; it would be dawn in a few hours.

Stace, Lev and Ethan sipped strong hot coffee in the warmth of the Harbormaster's office. Harcourt, the Harbormaster and a couple of his agents were also there.

"Okay, now we know the plan is for them to switch to a charter boat," Harcourt said, "As soon as they arrive at the drydock entrance, they'll disembark and head to the charter. And before anyone asks, yes, we've taken over the charter."

"What about the warehouse?" Lev asked.

Harcourt nodded, "Two SWAT teams are moving in as we speak."

"You're aware of the security cameras, I suppose."

"Yes, we're working the problem." Harcourt stretched his thin body and twisted his scrawny neck from side to side. "Tell me, Mr. Leventhal, what do you know about the security cameras?"

"If Tolomeo Technics manufactured them, they're good.

"In that case, for your own good, I'm ordering you three

off the dock and out of the area until this situation is over."

Lev pushed back his chair and stood holding his coffee mug. "Agent Harcourt, Ethan and I both recognize your position in all of this. Nonetheless, I'd like to make a suggestion."

Chapter 79

A wall-mounted chronometer clicked its minute hand to vertical. It was four in the morining. Twelve miles off shore from Seal Beach, Hank Tolomeo, his face a mask of determination, was at the controls of *Technocrat*, hands gripping the wheel as the craft rose and fell through the rough sea. New orders from Pashagora had reached him shortly after leaving Marina Del Rey.

Kate and Mel must to be set ashore at first light on State Beach in San Onofre, Orange County. A car would be waiting on Highway 5 to drive them to Ensenada, Mexico, and on to an airport, chosen for its remoteness. Hank held the twin diesels at full throttle.

Hank had heard that Vicky Vance had contacted Pashagora, informing him of the Stella/Chaz argument and break up. Understanding Pashagora's mind, he immediately recognized that such a split would alert too many people. Just how far would Pashagora go to ensure the silence of his American minions? Wouldn't he show some gratitude to them for their help? Hank Tolomeo hadn't gotten where he was today by believing in pipe dreams. He prepared for the worst.

He knew by now the US Coast Guard would be on the

lookout along the coast and around Long Beach/Seal Beach. He planned to remain 12 miles offshore until he reached the right coordinates, then make a fast run into San Onofre to put Kate and Mel ashore.

He'd checked the weather and it looked good, one to two foot swells with the wind from the East at five knots. Once he dropped off Mel, Kate and the computer equipment, he and Jilly would make a run for Ensenada, keeping to international waters.

Chapter 80

Lev set his coffee mug on the table. "Has it occurred to anyone that Hank Tolomeo's orders to come here and switch to a charter boat may have been changed since I was brought up to date by Stella Rae?" he asked looking hard at Harcourt. "If they have, we could all be wasting time."

Harcourt's head snapped up. "Clarify that remark."

"If I got the news about the rendezvous, it's possible others did, too, and while we continue waiting for Tolomeo to show and he could be going elsewhere."

"That's a possibility," Harcourt said begrudgingly. "I'll have the Harbormaster contact USCG and get an update on their search."

Before Harcourt could leave the room, a hand-held two-way radio on the table buzzed. He turned back and scooped it up. "Harcourt. Come in, over,"

"There are at least two people inside the building. We're moving in to reconnoiter the situation closer."

"Roger that, SWAT One," Harcourt switched off the radio and glanced questioningly at Lev.

A. G. Hayes

Chapter 81

Chaz Falconer generally played heroic parts in movies, but they used blanks in their automatic weapons. Scumbag was holding a Glock 17 under Chaz's chin and Chaz had no doubt that every one of the rounds in it were real.

Scumbag jerked his head toward the TV screen. "You tipped off the cops, didn't you, you dumb shit. Look."

Chaz moved his eyes to the screen and saw crouched figures moving toward the building. If he could break free, he'd have a chance of escape, but it was risky. Scumbag had been assigned to kill Jilly; he'd have no qualms in killing him, also. He could just make out several sticks of dynamite strapped together, with a taped timer attached, in the musty darkness beneath a crumbling stone stairway running from the main all the way to the top floor of the warehouse. The deadly device had been prepared by Scumbag who had bragged to Chaz that once he had Jilly back at the warehouse, he'd place her bound body beneath the staircase then remotely detonate the bomb, destroying any forensic evidence he might have left behind.

"We can still get away," Chaz wheezed.

"I didn't come here to get away. My job is to eliminate Jilly. If I fail, I'll be a dead man." He ordered Chaz to walk ahead, the barrel of his gun now inches from the back of Chaz's head, while he patted his shirt pocket to reassure himself that the remote detonator was still there.

Chaz forced himself to remember the last time he'd been in the warehouse. It had been daylight. Even then, the inside of the building was dark and gloomy in places. Huge overhead, beams ran from wall to wall. Parts of some of the upper floors had fallen away, rotted by rain and time. If he could break away from his captor, he'd have a slim chance of hiding amidst the rubble of the ruined building. That risk was counterbalanced by his knowledge that he'd never leave the structure alive if he didn't make an attempt. Physically, Chaz was in better shape than Scumbag. He just needed the right moment to make his move.

"Stop right there," Scumbag snarled. They were next to the dome-tent. Scumbag backed toward the tent, clearly wanting something from inside the tent. The Glock held steady in his right hand, he left felt back with his left for the tent opening. Chaz knew his moment had arrived.

"Hey! Someone's inside the tent!" Chaz yelled.

Scumbag reacted without thinking and turned to look. As he did, Chaz flew forward pushing Scumbag into the tent, and ripping one side of the flimsy tent across the entrance. His captor momentary entangled in the tent, Chaz kicked the Scumbag's outline hard in the back. The tent collapsed, entangling Scumbag like a fly in a spider web.

Two bullets ripped through the side of the tent missing Chaz by inches as he fled across the stone floor. Grabbing the bottom rung of an old iron ladder attached to the wall, he heaved himself up and continued climbing. Another shot sent brick splinters past his cheek as Scumbag struggled to get free.

Reaching an iron beam that had once been part of a truss holding the second floor; Chaz straddled it, and, carefully balancing himself, ran across it into the darkness. At the end, he arrived at the remains of the original wooden floor and gingerly rolled on to it, one hand on the iron beam in case the floor gave way. It held. Getting to his feet, he flattened as close to the brick wall as he could and continued shuffling deeper into the darkness.

Scumbag growled, grabbed a triple-X flashlight, and shined the beam upward. The light danced across the old brick walls and vanished in the black void above. "You're a dead man, dickhead! You'll never leave this place alive! I know every nook and cranny of this ancient pile of shit. There's no way you'll get away."

Chaz pressed against the wall and a brick rattled next to his hand. Gripping the loosened brick, he slowly withdrew it from the wall. He could hear Scumbag somewhere below, huffing and puffing in the darkness. Weighing the brick in his hand to get the feel, he tossed it toward the wall opposite from where he'd crossed the iron beam. He heard it hit something and rattle downward. A second later, he saw three flashes from the muzzle of Scumbag's automatic and heard three echoing shots.

"Dead man actor, you're playing your last part."

The stress in Scumbag's voice was apparent, giving Chaz a moment of hope. From the direction of the muzzle flashes, he had a good idea of his hunter's location. All the same, he remained stock-still, hardly breathing in the blackness.

The beam of the flashlight moved away from him and danced on the wall fifty feet in front of him, then flashed, one step at a time up the stone staircase. Scumbag was ascending it. Chaz could see the source of the beam slowly moving upward. It would only be a matter of time before they were on the same level. Chaz had to stop him.

With his back to the wall, Chaz edged along the outer rim of the wooden floor toward the spot where Scumbag would finally arrive at the top of the staircase. Inch by inch, every step a threat to his life if the floor sagged and collapsed, the two men slowly advanced toward a final destiny.

The old stone staircase that Scumbag was climbing had long ago lost its handrail to time and weather, leaving a drop of a hundred and twenty feet to the flagstones below. He continued steadily upward, the flashlight beam flickering across a three-foot length of rotted beam hanging like a broken tooth from the brick outer wall at the top of the stairs. Chaz saw it, too, and decided if he could loosen it and toss it down the stairs, he have a good chance of knocking the crazy bastard off the stairs.

Hearing Scumbag grunting from the climb, Chaz moved fast. At the top of the stairs, Chaz grasped the beam. Pieces of plaster showered around him and the beam loosen almost at once. For the moment, he had to hold it in place to get his footing more secure. Slowly, he lowered the beam toward his shoulder. It was heavier than he thought, and the end tipped forward, pulling Chaz off balance just as Scumbag came into view.

The flashlight beam caught Chaz in a black and white tableau of horror as he and the beam pitched forward. The tip of the timber beam smashed into Scumbag's face with a loud crunch and both men went off the stairs in a rattle of loose bricks. Scumbag hit the ground first. In the shower of debris, a piece of brick pressed the wireless detonator in his shirt pocket, and a thunderous explosion brought down the ancient stone staircase creating a mountain of rubble thirty feet high.

Chapter 82

Harcourt updated Lev and the others that the SWAT teams had heard gunshots from inside the warehouse followed by an explosion and now considered it unsafe to enter. It would be some time before further details became available.

A Coast Guard cutter sailing between Long Beach and Seal Beach received a message from Harcourt updating them on the warehouse explosion, suggesting the possibility that the information about the yacht being in the area was no longer correct.

"So what happens now?" asked Ethan. "Are they going to go home and forget it?"

"No, sir," Harcourt said. "The search will continue north and south along the coast. Rest assured the yacht will be found."

"I'm concerned about my daughter, not the yacht," Ethan grumbled.

"Of course, I understand. The Office of Homeland Security will continue the investigation using every available resource."

"That's fine, and in the meantime, we're supposed to just

wait around?" Ethan asked petulantly.

Stace exchanged looks with Lev who suggested the three get some breakfast, then reconsider their part in the unfolding drama.

As Stace buttered her toast, Ethan said, "Why do I get the feeling we've been played for suckers? That phone call you got from, what's-her-name…"

"Stella Rae," Lev said.

"Yeah, she could have been ordered to give you a false lead allowing the yacht time to head somewhere else."

"That's true, but somehow I believe she was telling the truth. If someone found out she alerted us, then yes, the plan could have been changed."

"So the yacht with Kate aboard could be sailing south as we sit here eating breakfast," Ethan quickly added.

Lev pushed the remains of a fried egg to the side of his plate, cut a piece of toast in half and wondered if Ethan was right.

"If what Stella said was true—and I, too, believe it so—we're at least in the right place to hear if something breaks," Stace said. "It's not even daylight yet. The Coast Guard is doing their job and Harcourt said he'd let us know as soon as he had any information. I say we hang around here awhile and see what develops."

With reluctance, Ethan had to agreed.

Chapter 83

Tolomeo was holding steady on the corrected coordinates. Daybreak was still an hour away. He'd take them ashore in the inflatable at first light. Kate had remained in her bunk throughout the journey, unable to sleep due to the rough seas and seasickness, but he guessed she'd probably overheard the others discussing what to do next.

"Show time in fifteen minutes, Jilly," Hank called.

Jilly went below. "We're almost there, Kate. Get your stuff together. The moment Hank drops anchor, you and Mel must be on your way, so Hank and I can head back into international waters."

Kate followed Jill onto the main deck and sat cradling the computer case in her arms as Mel and Jilly unlashed the inflatable. The yacht was rapidly nearing its drop point and Kate shook with a combination of seasickness and apprehension. Anyone who glanced at her would conclude that she was far too weak to cry out or escape.

Mel carried an outboard motor across the deck, installed it on the transom of the inflatable dingy, and immediately began stowing his and Kate's personal belongings, including the laptop and Al Jolson in a canvas sea bag. Finished, Mel attempted to cheer Kate up. "Kate, look at it this way: We were going to be married and join my family in India. Nothing's really changed."

"You must be out of your mind, Melhi Pashagora! *Everything* has changed," she lashed out. "You and your father were plotting to get my program from the start. I've never meant anything to you!"

Mel stared down at her, shrugged and turned away. "Then look at it another way: You're lucky you're still alive, Kate."

"Make ready to drop anchor, Jilly, when I give the order." Hank watched his gauge until he could confirm the right depth, then switched off the engines and called out, "Weigh anchor!"

Jilly stood in the bow and lowered the Danforth anchor over the side, the thick coil of line unwound then stopped as the anchor bit into the sandy bottom of State Beach. The yacht immediately swung slightly to port and the line tightened. They'd arrived. Hank looked over his shoulder to the East as the first streaks of light broke low on the horizon.

"Okay people, let's move," Hank yelled, handing the helm over to Jilly and going forward to help slide the inflatable over the side. "Keep the line secure, Jilly."

Once in the water, Hank climbed aboard and primed the outboard motor. Mel brought Kate to the dingy and held her arm as she stepped aboard.

"Sit there," Hank ordered Kate, pointing to the center of the craft, "and don't move about."

Mel lowered the sea bag aboard and followed. Hank yanked the starter cord and the outboard came alive on the first pull. Adjusting the throttle, he headed for the beach. The morning air was cold and he could taste salt on his lips. In the distance, he heard the sound of breakers hitting the shore.

Less than five minutes later, they rode a wave onto the beach. Mel jumped out taking the line and holding the boat for Kate to follow. Hank heaved the sea bag in an arc onto the beach and waved for Mel to let loose of the line. Opening the throttle, Hank urged the dingy forward into the waves.

Mel grabbed the sea bag and Kate's hand and tugged her across the beach to Highway 5. Still too dark to see much, he swiveled his head both ways looking for the pickup vehicle. The highway was empty.

Hank made it back to the yacht under his estimated time limit. He and Jilly pulled the inflatable on deck and, as Jilly tied it down, he had the yacht under power and heading back out to beyond the twelve-mile limit.

"We're on our own now, Jilly," Hank rasped.

"Why didn't you just refuse Pashagora's new orders? We had everything we needed: his son, Kate and the program. He'd have had to let the original plan stand."

"Jilly, we are back to the original plan. Kumar wanted to

be certain Kate and the program arrived in Mumbai. That always was the plan. Too many people came to know of it, so things had to be changed, but minimally, subtly, so that he could still take advantage all the arrangements he'd made."

Jilly snorted, "Yeah. And that includes leaving us to run the risk of being captured by the US Coast Guard."

Hank notched up the engines and headed southeast; it was getting lighter by the minute. He told Jilly to make a pot of fresh coffee.

On shore, Mel paced beside the highway as the sound of the outboard faded.

"Seems your friends got lost or have abandoned you," Kate said looking up and down the vacant road.

"I don't think so. My father doesn't hire fools." He removed a cell phone from his pocket snapped it open and saw they were in a no reception zone.

Chapter 84

Achy breaky Heart twanged from the dashboard speaker of the battered '74 Dodge van as it cruised along Highway 5. Jack Alard and Zeek Fell sang along with the music. Jack was driving.

"Well lookie there, Zeek, will ya?" Ahead, two figures stood at the side of the highway, a canvas sea bag between them.

The old Dodge squealed to a halt. "The red head looks good. You can have t'other one, Zeek."

Jack and Zeek were on their way to Mexico with twenty dollars between them; the two strangers beside an empty highway looked like an ATM machine to them.

Zeek rolled down the window and gave a snaggletooth grin. "Morning folks, you need a ride, I reckon."

Even in the half-light of early dawn, Kate knew they were bad news. Her seasickness had abated sufficiently for her to feel her skin prickle with alert tension.

"No problem," Mel said. "We're being picked up. But thanks for the offer."

"'Taint no problem, boy." Zeek pulled out and pointed a Colt Forty-five at them. "Jest open that there side door and climb in." He waved the revolver side to side. "This here's the gun won the West, or so my granddaddy used to say. Show some respect. Get your asses in the truck. Now." Kate knew that if they got in the vehicle, they'd likely never get out.

"Hey! Whoa!" Mel said. "I'll give you some money if you beat it." His eyebrows narrowed and his fingers did a nervous tap-dance against his leg.

"How much you got, boy?"

"A couple of thousand," Mel said.

Zeeks eyes widened, "American dollars?"

"Yes, of course."

"How about the little lady, how much she got?"

"About twenty bucks," Kate replied.

"Okay, tell you what. You, young fella, give me the two thousand dollars and you can stay and wait for your ride. Red Head comes with us. She can make up her two thousand in one way or another." Zeek leered at Kate and grinned.

A car zoomed past, definitely not driven by a Good Samaritan. The van swayed in its backwash.

It was growing lighter and Zeek acted antsy. Billy Ray Cyrus was still singing, "'And if you tell my heart, my achy breaky heart, he might blow up and kill this man'. Oooo."

Kate's eyes glinted for a moment as she imagined Mel spattered across Highway 5 by the gun that won the West. "I think our ride is here," Kate said, pointing back in the direction from where the truck had come. Zeek twisted his scrawny neck to glance back, and Mel was on him with the speed of a striking cobra, wresting the revolver from his grasp.

Mel fired one shot into the side of the van. "Okay, you can drive away or stay and wait for the CHPs and file a complaint. It's up to you." Like father like son.

"Pick up the bag, Mel," Kate hissed. "It's yours if you give me the gun. I'll take their truck. Hurry."

Mel looked up and down the road, wanting to keep the gun and discover their prearranged ride. In the end, he decided the sea bag with its computer equipment was most important. Let Kate take care of herself. He grabbed the bag, trotted back down the road about twenty feet and tossed her the gun. Kate caught it in the air, opened the side door of the van, climbed inside and aimed the gun at Jack, the driver.

"Move out fast and keep looking straight ahead. My granddaddy had one of these Peacemakers, and taught me how to use it when I was ten years old." Jack and Zeek heard the hammer click back and stared straight ahead, the van gathering speed.

Checking his rearview mirror, Jack said, "Hey, that guy you were with is just staring at us. Well, whadduya know? The jerk is smiling. Now he's looking t'other way, prob'ly for that lost car of his."

The country western song, *Refried Beans*, had replaced *Achy Breaky Heart*, and was playing at full blast. "Turn that off. I can't hear myself think," Kate ordered. Zeek leaned forward and obeyed.

"Keep driving till I tell you, then stop. Let me out and you can continue on your way."

"What about my granddaddy's forty-five?" Zeek asked, still staring straight ahead. Kate looked at the untidy mess these two most likely called home. "When I leave, I'll put it under your mattress."

"You sure you wouldn't like to join us, Red Head?" Zeek wheezed. "I kinda like yer style. We could make a U-turn, go back and get the money off your boyfriend there. With his two thousand and your twenty we could live high on the hog in Mexico."

"Don't think so. We'll do this my way." Kate paused. "Do either of you have a cell phone?"

"Nope," Jack said. "Neither of us knows anyone to call, and besides, Zeek is hard of hearing." Zeek laughed nervously at Jack's joke.

As the sun rose higher in the East, the highway 5 became easier to see. Kate peered ahead hoping to see a public rest stop or mobile border checkpoint; they could appear anywhere, or for sure, at the USMC base at Camp Pendelton, two miles away according to the most recent sign.

"Unless I tell you otherwise, take the Camp Pendelton turnoff. Same drill. I'll say you gave me a lift, and then you guys can move on."

"Marines don't care for our sort," Zeek growled.

"Yeah, well, don't worry about it, fellas. The Marines won't care about you two." Kate prayed she'd get to Pendelton safely. That way she could get word to Lev and agent Harcourt.

A. G. Hayes

Chapter 85

Standing with the sea bag at his side, Mel tried hitching a ride. Someone was going to pay for this fuck-up. Several cars passed before a black BMW came to a stop. The passenger door opened and a tall thin man got out, his eyes reflecting concern. "Mr. Pashagora?"

Mel felt like punching the man in the face. "Where the hell have you been?"

"It couldn't be helped, sir. We had a flat. I tried but couldn't raise you on your cell."

"Put that in the trunk, we've lost valuable time," Mel ordered. The tall man hurriedly stowed the sea bag, opened the back passenger door for Mel, then returned to his seat next to the driver.

"Step on it!" Mel yelled. "We have to catch up with an old Dodge van. They have a fifteen minute lead, so move it!"

Kate saw the Camp Pendleton turnoff sign, and said, "There! Hang a left." She ordered, jabbing the nozzle of the .45 in the direction of the turnoff. The van slowed, turning and following in the direction the gun was pointed.

"When we get to the gate, do like I said. I'll tell them you gave me a lift. You turn around and leave. End of story."

When the van came to a stop, Kate was out the side door faster than the Marine guard walking toward them.

"They gave me a lift," she jerked her thumb over her shoulder. "I must speak to the camp commander. It's a matter of life and death."

Jack immediately backed up the truck, made a three point turn and wisked away, the radio blaring out a new country and western song.

Chapter 86

Harcourt received a call from the Camp Pendelton Commandant's office inquiring about a Miz Kate Keenan. Harcourt brought Pendelton up to date explaining she was an important part of an ongoing joint OHS/NSA investigation and requested clearance for a helicopter to land at Pendelton and fly her to the Federal building in Westwood for questioning.

Kate was safe. Harcourt contacted the Coast Guard and updated them, assuring them that although they had Kate in possession, the search for the yacht and its occupants should continue.

Within minutes of the helicopter landing on the pad atop the Federal building, Kate was hustled to a secure debriefing room where Harcourt and several other personal from the FBI and the NSA awaited

"Please sit down Ms. Keenan." Harcourt indicated an empty chair at one end of a highly polished oval conference table. Two men and a middle-aged woman were already seated.

Kate, exhausted from her ordeal, dropped into the chair, brushing her fingers through her tangled red hair. She looked up as a cup of coffee was set beside her.

"That will be all," Harcourt said, dismissing the woman who had brought in the coffee. "Now, Miz Keenan, I'd like to introduce you to everyone at the table. My name is Agent Harcourt, FBI, working with the OHS, the Office of Homeland Security. The lady on your right is Agent Pritchard, FBI." Kate glanced at her and nodded. Harcourt continued, "Facing her, Agents Richardson and Falk, National Security Agency." Agent Falk, lean, with chestnut hair falling towards his eyebrows, rustled his notes and Kate studied at him. For some reason, Harcourt noticed, Kate's gaze sharpened at Falk's presence. Harcourt cleared his throat. Kate looked back at him and nodded.

"As you are aware, NSA, the National Security Agency, indicated an interest in your computer program when you attended a job interview some time ago." Kate remained silent.

"Now, Miz Keenan, the government is more than just interested. Your program has been reclassified top secret. As you well know, your life is in jeopardy. Those responsible for the actions taken against you over the last few days are being pursued and, when apprehended, will be brought to justice."

Kate took a sip of her coffee, holding the saucer in her left hand beneath the cup, like a Duchess at afternoon tea. Setting the cup and saucer on the table, she glanced again at Falk, then addressed Harcourt.

"I see. The government will of course, pay for the honor

of keeping my program out of circulation?"

Harcourt was at a loss for words. Agent Falk sat straighter in his chair. NSA Agent Richardson's ruddy face got redder as he spluttered, "Miz Keenan. We're talking national security here."

"I understand," Kate acknowledged. "However, you must understand that more than my physical security—my fiscal security is also at risk. I designed the program for civilian use in the entertainment sector. That alone would make me financially independent. If the government wants to use my program for military purposes, then they will have to pay for it."

Agent Richardson narrowed his eyes. "Then we will have to take this to a higher level, Miz Keenan."

"Yes. As high as it takes." She pushed back her chair and stood, fingertips spread lightly on the edge of the table. "Am I free to go then, Agent Harcourt? If so, I would like to make a phone call to have someone pick me up."

"I must warn you Miz Keenan, you will be in mortal danger the moment you leave the building."

"Yes, but then, I was in danger before you brought me here. Remember, *I* called *you*. Your organizations together have been unable to find me for over a week. I'll take my chances, at least until we can come to a reasonable agreement. Oh, and if you're worried about the computer, don't. The password was only good for twenty-four hours. "

A. G. Hayes

Chapter 87

Lev decided they would wait until daylight, and if they heard nothing from Harcourt, they'd return to Hollywood. Daylight had arrived, and the trio headed for home in a somber mood.

Lev's cell chimed as he approached downtown Los Angeles on the Santa Anna Freeway. "Yes, this is he."

Stace saw his face brighten and asked, "Who is it?"

Lev ignored her, concentrating on the call. "You're with Harcourt at the Federal Building? That's great news!" His smile faded as he continued to listen. "Well, I'm sure everything will work out. Yes, I can there within the hour." He flipped the phone shut. "Kate's safe and sound at the Federal Building in Westwood. We're to pick her up."

"Thank God!" Ethan exclaimed. "How did Harcourt find them?"

"He didn't. Kate called him from Camp Pendelton." Lev made the transition onto the Hollywood Freeway and headed west.

"What happened to her abductors?" Ethan asked.

"We'll find out when we see her." Lev's voice had a lilt of relief in it, and the atmosphere in the car lightened considerably.

Lev, Ethan and Stace cleared security at the Federal Building, were issued plastic visitor ID tags to place around their necks and told to continue to the fourteenth floor. Harcourt was waiting beside the door of the elevator when it slid open.

"Where is she?" were the first words out of Ethan's mouth when he saw Harcourt.

"Follow me," Harcourt growled and led them to the debriefing room. Kate was alone at the table. The others had left.

Ethan rushed across the room and hugged her. "You all right, Baby? How did you get away?"

"I'm fine, Dad." She looked over his shoulder at Lev and Stace. "I'm glad you're here. It's a long story. I'll fill you in when we get home."

Harcourt cut in. "Miz Keenan, again I must warn you that you will be in mortal danger without government protection. We are well aware of Kumar Pashagora, a man of seemingly unlimited wealth and power with the ability to give orders in Mumbai and, within hours, have them carried out here in the United States."

"Then why wasn't government protection given to her earlier?" Ethan rasped.

"Her kidnapping at the studio happened before we were

aware of the extent of the Pashagora organization," Harcourt snapped.

Lev and Ethan exchanged glances. "Are you suggesting the government offer my daughter some sort of 'bodyguard service'?" Ethan asked.

Harcourt shook his head. "Not exactly, sir. It is absolutely important that Miz Keenan be kept in a safe location until we have secured all of Pashagora's players."

"What happened to her computer, Harcourt?" Lev asked. Harcourt glanced at Kate before answering.

"Miz Keenan stated that Kumar's son has it, along with Al Jolson. Oh, yes, we've know about Al for some time, Mr. Leventhal."

"And the government wants to keep my client in a safe house until they've captured all of Pashagora's men and have the computer in their care?"

"That is our—my—suggestion."

"Well, when I last checked, we were living in a free country. Let's ask Kate what she would like to do."

"Get me out of here, Lev. Dad and I will be fine. Pashagora's men can't use the computer. The password has expired. If they try to force it, it'll disintegrate before their eyes."

Harcourt shrugged, his thin body rigid with anger. "Very well, Miz Keenan, so be it." Despite Harcourt's acquiescence,

Lev knew they hadn't heard the end of it by any means.

Lev drove along Wilshire Boulevard, heading towards Kate's house in West Hollywood. "Maybe you should have taken the government's offer more seriously, Kate," Stace offered.

Kate shook her head. "Not right now. First I want to check my mail, get a few things together, then Ethan and I will find a good hotel for a couple of days."

"You can both stay with me. I have plenty of room," Stace urged.

"She's right, Kate," Lev said quickly. "There's safety in numbers. He parked in the driveway, recalling the last time he'd been there. It seemed an age ago.

Kate stared at the house. "I'm glad to be home. Come on in. We'll make some coffee and I'll tell you what happened."

Twenty minutes later, after Kate finished her story, Lev was the first to ask a question. "So Mel has the computer and Al Jolson. What happens now?"

"Correction, Lev. Mel *thinks* he has everything. He and his dad are in for a shock when they try to make use of it." Kate had a sudden thought. "Hey! I didn't check my snail mail."

Kate walked to the hall and picked up a pile of mail scattered on the floor. "There it is." She pulled a slim package from the letters and held it for all to see.

"You mean…" Lev began,

"Yeah, Lev, I mailed the real Al Jolson home for safety and substituted a fake one just in case."

"But I carried it with me all the time we were in Nevada, until returning to my office," Lev said.

"You left your jacket draped over the back of a chair in your room at Binion's. I made the switch while you, Mel and Dad were in deep conversation about the Hollywood rumor mill while we waited for room service."

"Wait! Where did you find a fake Al Jolson?"

"I took the real one out of your jacket and replaced it with my iPod wrapped in toilet paper. It fit perfectly into the envelope you were carrying it in. Before we left the hotel, I took the real Al Jolson to the front desk and had them box and mail it first class to my house. Here it is, safe and sound."

Lev was dumbfounded. "You took a big gamble, Kate."

"Hey, we went to Vegas and never even dropped a quarter in a slot machine. I did what most people do when they go to Las Vegas. I took a chance."

"So Mel has a computer set to destroy itself if anyone tries to mess with it, an iPod, and an expired password," Ethan said quietly. "When Kumar Pashagora finds out, it might be wise to be under government protection, Baby."

Stacy suddenly said, "Looks like the government has sent you some mail already, Kate."

Lev saw what she was referring to, reached down, and retrieved a buff colored official looking envelope. "It's from the United States Patent office, Kate," he said with a smile.

Chapter 88

The BMW zoomed past Camp Pendelton a minute before the Dodge van returned onto Highway 5.

Mel squinted into the sun, trying to spot the decrepit Dodge van in the thickening morning traffic as they approached Oceanside. The BMW steadily widened the gap as the Dodge trundled behind them.

A. G. Hayes

Chapter 89

The pushing currents rushed Hank Tolomeo and Jilly Suede closer to their Mexican destination, Ensenada. Suddenly, the jangling sound of the satellite phone sounded. Hank's ear was immediately assailed by the angry voice of Kumar Pashagora, informing him of Kate's escape and the need for yet another change in plans.

"You understand, Tolomeo, that had it not been for quick work on the part of my son, we would have lost everything again. Follow my new orders to the letter." The phone went dead.

Jilly had seen the anger rise on Hank's face as he listened to the call. "What was that about?"

"Damn Pashagora's altering plans again."

"Why? What happened?"

Hank pulled a chart toward him, his eyes flickering across the instrument panel then back to the chart. "That little shit Kate escaped. She's gone. Mel has the complete computer system. Pashagora's wants us to rendezvous with a Mexican trawler out of Ensenada. We're to transfer aboard. A couple of the crew will sail my yacht further down the coast to a remote fishing village."

"If we rendezvous, what's to stop them from killing us, Hank? Pashagora has everything he needs. We're a liability now."

"Tell me about it, Jilly."

"What are we going to do?"

Hank throttled back on the engines, checked the amount of fuel remaining in the tanks and made a fast decision. "We're going to Marina Costa Baja. The La Paz region of Mexico. I can sell the yacht for cash there, then we can decide where to go. In the meantime, while we're still in the Satellite footprint, we're going to retransfer our money from the bank in Mumbai to an offshore investment corporation I know in Jersey. Get the papers. We need to do it now."

Time differences, normally a problem for domestic banks, were no problem for the international banking community, especially offshore banks acting as tax havens. Jilly handled the phone and paper work while Hank plotted a new course. Less than an hour later, they were sailing in an area where the Mexican fishing boat would never locate them; and their bank accounts now had new homes in the Channel Islands.

Chapter 90

The US government had ears all over the world. Several people, high in Mumbai business circles, had received coded messages alerting them of the US govenrment's need to know a great deal more about Kumar Pashagora's activities.

One of those who received a message was Pradeep Kurade, a short, soft-spoken, middle-aged man with an office in Cuffe Parade, an important business district of Mumbai.

Pradeep worked as an analyst for the Indian government documenting the growth and progress of the Indian Film Industry, a perfect cover in a city such as Mumbai where life was fast, growth unparalleled, action unconstrained. In short, a dream hoards of young Indians wanting to become instant millionaires. Of course, few ever did. Most eventually ended up in the gutters of Calcutta, or worse, dead. In Kurade's case, that was not so. He had a direct line to NSA.

Rick Richardson, the ruddy faced NSA agent replaced his secure phone to its cradle. "The word is out in Mumbai. One man in particular will, I'm sure, be able to get us the background information we need."

Harcourt grunted. "But will he be able to get hold of the computer?"

"Put it this way, Harcourt. I've already got people in place who working on that problem. Time will tell."

"Yes, however, in the meantime, we have to be sure we have Keenan covered. If Pashagora's people get her, that'll be the end of it."

"She's covered," replied Richardson.

Chapter 91

Kate scooped up the rest of the mail, quickly checked through it, then set it aside and announced, "I've thought of something, Lev. I have a key to Mel's apartment on Shoreham. Let's check it out now that we know what he really wanted."

"Good idea, Kate, and you know what? Maybe you should stay at his place. They have top security there."

"The apartment is large—three bedrooms with an office—and, yes, security is excellent. But how do we let management know I'll be staying there without tipping of the Pashagoras?"

"I'll make a couple of discrete calls," Lev said. "It's possible no one here is aware that Mel's left town."

A few "discrete" calls later, Lev announced, "Looks like things are finally going our way. Everyone I contacted thinks Mel is still here in Hollywood."

"Do you remember his apartment number, Kate?"

"Sure, twelve-oh-eight," Kate shot back. "I've been there enough times over the last couple of years."

"Even better. You won't seem a stranger to the doorman." Lev checked the yellow pages and phoned the desk at the

Shoreham Towers. The phone rang twice before it was picked up.

"Yes. Good evening. My name is Lev Leventhal," Lev said nonchalantly. "I was just speaking to Mr Pashagora, and he asked me to call and convey a message to his fiancé, Ms. Kate Keenan. Would you connect me please?"

"Mr. Pashagora is away at the moment, and Ms. Keenan isn't here."

"Yes, I know he's away. That's why he asked me to speak to his fiancé. She'll be staying there until he returns sometime next week."

"Oh, yes. But I'm afraid she's not arrived yet. However, I can give her your message when she arrives."

"No, that's all right, she's probably getting together a few things to take with her to the apartment. A couple of her friends are picking her up and driving her over. No doubt there's a lot of luggage. You know the way women are."

"Yes, sir. I'll be here at the desk when she arrives. My name is David."

"Thank you, David." Lev grinned impishly at Kate and closed his cell. "Well, it doesn't seem Mel or his father has canceled the lease. Let's hide you in the lion's den. Okay with you, Stace?"

Stace nodded, "Sure, as long as I get a bedroom of my own."

"Fine, Ethan and I will notify Harcourt, although, I'll bet he'll know where Kate is within five minutes of when you arrive at the apartment."

David greeted them with a smile and a good word, and several minutes later they were in apartment 1208.

Ethan surveyed the view. "Wow, Mel really lives big. This is a lot better than my place in Arizona."

Stace paced the living room looking at the furnishings with a practiced eye. "There's several glasses that have been used recently. Where did he keep his papers and things like that, I wonder?"

"Come, Stace. I'll show you. He has an office."

Kate opened a door at the end of the hall to reveal chrome and leather office furniture, track lighting, a bank of computer screens and two telephones, the red one, a satellite phone. Stace was about to speak when Kate grabbed her arm and walked her out of the office.

"What's wrong, Kate?" Stace asked. Kate shook her head, held a finger to her lips, and whispered, "He's installed a video camera since I was last here. I saw the glint of a lens in the crown molding."

"So we're on tape and maybe also on someone's silver screen somewhere, too." Stace looked worried. "What do we do now?"

We'll walk back in and act as if we're looking for some

papers. If I know Mel, he'll have everything recorded and transmitted every fifteen minutes. We find it and disable it. Get Lev and Ethan in here. We have to be fast."

Methodically, the four checked out the office and five minutes into the search, Ethan whispered, "I've found it." The small recorder was hidden inside a sliding panel in the closet.

"Neat installation," Ethan muttered, "a built-in cubbyhole. And the recorder is connected to a satellite cable. Here's a transmission schedule tapped next to it. We've got ten minutes before the next transmission."

"Very professional," Lev agreed as he switched the unit off, removed the disk, and asked, "Anyone find anything else of interest?

"These." Kate slapped a collection of head shots onto the desktop. Five had a red slash drawn diagonally across. "The ones with a red slash means they're dead," Kate said slowly. "Look, these others are of us. I don't recognize a number of the others, do you?"

Lev studied the photographs, then abruptly said, "We're leaving. Bring the pictures, Kate. We're going to the Federal Building right now. Harcourt will be interested in this rogues' gallery. Besides, it means Mel might have given his apartment keys to his father's goons."

Chapter 92

It was midmorning when the BMW dropped Mel off at Mexico City's Benito Juárez International Airport. He purchased a decent piece of carryon luggage, a new shirt, a jacket, a pair of Italian leather loafers and a pair of slacks. In the men's room, he transferred the computer to the carryon, stuffed his old clothes into the sea bag, and dumped the bag into a trash bin.

After cleaning up, he checked the new Indian passport and first class ticket on British Airways to Mumbai, with stops in Chicago O'Hare and London Heathrow, that his contact in the BMW had supplied him.

Thirty crisp new one hundred-dollar bills tucked neatly in the back of the ticket holder completed his accoutrements. His flight was due to leave after noon, 12:44 to be precise. He had two days of peaceful flying ahead of him.

A. G. Hayes

Chapter 93

As Harcourt entered the room, Richardson hung up the phone. "One of our people called from Mexico City International Airport. Mel Pashagora is due to leave on a British Airways/AeroMexicana flight at twelve forty-four hours in the afternoon, arriving at Chicago O'Hare at fourteen fifty-five hours Eastern Standard Time.

"Good work. We'll be waiting. He'll never clear customs. We'll take him on home ground and have the US Marshals haul his sorry ass back here to LA."

Richardson's intercom announced a Ms. Keenan and party had just arrived carrying important information.

Harcourt reached across and pressed a button,."Send them up."

The four visitors were directed to main conference room in the Federal Building. Harcourt was standing; Richardson speaking. "These photographs," NSA Agent Richardson spread them across the table and aligned the pictures of Frank Primo, Charles Vance, Don Ames, Franz Villand and Chaz Falconer into a single row, creating second row of unrecognized faces beneath the first, "are very helpful. Three with red slashes were murdered by unknown assailants, one in an explosion and Villand shot dead by a hit squad outside of your office, Mr. Leventhal. Is that right?"

Lev nodded. "That's correct."

Richardson arched his eyebrows and tapped Ames' red slashed photo.

"This man was found dead on your doorstep, I believe."

"Yes, he was. I wasn't at home at the time."

"I know. You, Ms. Keenan and her father were wandering around Nevada after having been instructed by Agent Harcourt not to leave town."

"We've been through all that, Agent Richardson. We came here to help, not to rehash past events."

Richardson ignored the remark, and rearragned the pictures into two rows, one of the men, the other of the women. "Well, Miz Kate Keenan and Miz Stacy Hart, I know where you are at the moment. What about the others here, any idea?"

"At home, I would imagine," Stacy said quietly.

"You're all acquainted with the women?" Richardson waved a beefy hand over the collection.

"Yes, but my Dad never actually met Stella Rae. She came to LA after he left town several years ago."

Harcourt cut in. "You found nothing else in Pashagora's apartment that might be of use to us?"

"No," Kate slid a key across the table. "Here check the

apartment for yourselves. You won't even have to use a lock pick this time. We brought you the pictures and the tape. That's all we found. It looked like some people had possibly been visiting, and, what with the photos and active video surveillance equipment, Lev thought it wise for us to leave as quickly as possible."

Harcourt bristled for a moment, and then gave a thin smile, remembering his bosses had ordered that he maintain a "good working relationship" with Ms. Kate Keenan.

"We'll get in touch with these ladies, and work on identifying the rest of the men."

Lev pushed back from the table and asked Harcourt, "Any news on the yacht or where Mel Pashagora might be?"

"Nothing yet. However, we're following a couple of leads. I'll let you know when we something more definite."

Richardson glanced at Harcourt, then asked Kate, "What made you decide to go to Pashagora's apartment anyway?"

"You did, actually," she replied.

"Me?" Richardson grated.

"What exactly are you saying, Miz Keenan?" asked Harcourt.

"Both of you advised us to be careful. That we could be watched. That our lives would be in danger."

"Yes, and we suggested you accept our offer of governmental protection and you walked out on the idea."

"I feel you two have been making more of an effort to get my computer program than to provide for my safety, Agent Richardson." She paused before turning to Harcourt. "You had your people check out the apartment before we got there, didn't you?"

"Of course," Harcourt replied.

"Why didn't you take the photos and tape?"

"You know, Ms. Keenan, it's we who usually ask the questions. Nevertheless, we made copies of the photos and left the originals. As for the hidden recorder, we weren't looking for it."

"We wanted to see what you would do when you found the pictures," added Richardson.

"You didn't know the office was being monitored?" asked Ethan.

"I didn't say that. You're welcome to return to the apartment. It's been thoroughly gone over. As for its security, NSA added substantially to it."

Harcourt opened the door. "We'll keep in touch."

"Could you drop me off at a car rental agency, Lev?" Ethan asked as the four filed out, stunned by what they'd heard. "Your car is known to too many. Leave your car in the driveway. I'll rent a car, park it down the hill, and call you. Then send Stace down. I'll have her rent a second car and, from then on, one can watch the other's tail."

Chapter 94

Hank slept a couple of hours with the yacht on autopilot. Jilly remained close to the helm; she was no sailor, but she could awaken Hank if an emergency arose. Sitting in complete blackness except for the soft green glow of the instrument panel, she checked the chronometer: 3:30 a.m.

The soft thud-thud of the engines and the splash of the sea against the hull were the only sounds. Jilly wondered if she had made the right decision to go on this crazy escapade. Hank drove her nuts at times, but at least he always had a plan for their next move.

Hank's voice jolted her out of her revere, "Everything okay?" He quickly scanned the instrument panel.

"Damn it, Hank! You scared the hell out of me, creeping up like that."

"Who were you expecting? There's only the two of us on board."

"I was miles away," Jilly grumbled.

"Yeah, well, we need a few more between us and the Coast Guard before I'll have time for daydreams of my own."

"I was thinking of our future, Hank. What are we going to do?"

"Did you ever hear of Lord Lucan?"

"The name sounds vaguely familiar, why?"

"He killed a woman in London back in 1974. He escaped capture and has never been found."

"What has that to do with us, Hank?"

"It proves to me that if high profile people like Lord Lucan can vanish and never to be heard of again, so can we."

"So we're going to commit ourselves to a life on the run, forever having to look back over our shoulders? Remember, one of the guys who did the great train robbery and escaped from prison in England? He hid out in Rio for years. They eventually found him."

"They did, and couldn't extradite him back to the UK. He returned forty years later on his own accord. He was promptly sent back to prison."

"You seem to know a lot about people who run, Hank."

"I work in Hollywood, where movies of hideous horrors and astounding escapes are commonplace. Anyway don't you worry, no one will find us. We have money and brains."

"Make that cunning and ruthlessness, Hank, and I'll believe you."

Hank chuckled, and pushed the throttles forward and the yacht came to life, its bow rising as he set the speed at a steady twenty-five knots.

Chapter 95

Ethan rented a low profile car, phoned Lev, and told him to put Stace on. "Hi, Stace. Now listen carefully: Meet me at Oakstone Way and Lookout Mountain. I'm driving a green Echo. Oakstone's about a quarter mile down from Lev's place."

"An Echo?" Stace repeated.

"Folksy," Ethan muttered.

"Sure is. I know where Oakstone is." She closed the cell and turned to Lev. "He's in a green Echo."

Lev grinned, "Better than a blue funk. Call me from the car rental office, okay?"

"Yes, and don't tell me what to rent." She waved to Kate and left.

Stace signed for a steel gray Toyota Corolla, called Lev and drove off the lot followed by Ethan's green Echo.

Twenty minutes later, Stace was raising her voice to be heard over the noise and constant clatter of dishes. She and Ethan were sitting at a table for two in Denny's Hollywood.

"Lev lives at one of the most difficult addresses to find in all of Hollywood. Narrow winding roads. Make one wrong turn and you end up driving a mile before you discover it's a dead end and have to drive back again." She sighed. "Why doesn't he sell the place?"

"That's why he's been able to last so long in Hollywood. Every night he comes home to quiet and solitude."

"Yeah, so did Harry Bosch and look what it got him."

Ethan smiled at her reference to one of Mike Connelly's character heroes. "Perhaps the narrow winding roads will help Kate and him to get away from the house without being seen."

Stace nodded, "If they are being watched."

"I'm sure NSA will have tabs on them and maybe Pashagora's people, too."

"But why would his people bother now they have the computer?"

Ethan hesitated to answer, then, choosing discretion, shrugged. "I'll be on the watch, until I know that answer."

"You should have been a cop, Ethan."

"Yeah, and if I had, I'd be retired and not in this mess."

"Then maybe we wouldn't have met up again, Ethan." She reached across the table and touched his hand. He encircled her hand with his, and gave it a loving squeeze.

"You're right there, Stace," he said, his hand lingering over hers.

Chapter 96

Mel shuffled toward O'Hare Customs doing his best to appear bored. He mentally checked everything as the line inched forward. Passport. He knew it looked perfect, but would it pass the high tech scrutiny of today's technology? Three thousand in cash should be no problem. They only investigated people carrying over ten thousand. The computer was an ordinary laptop; it would pass with no problem. Inside the extra box would be what appear to be specially designed iPad or such.

A voice behind him murmured, "Would you come with us, sir? This way, please."

Two suited men led him out of line toward a special room. Mel's blood felt like it was draining from his brain and he experienced a feeling of lightheadedness. He sagged and his stride faltered. The two men supported him and continued walking. He didn't attempt to resist.

The special room was claustrophobic and smelled of collected fear and tension. Lev was made to sit at in a chair at a table, both bolted to the floor. He was informed that they knew who he was, and told him he was being sent back to Los Angeles for interrogation. Mel rehearsed in his mind several explanations, but they asked no questions. In LA, on familiar ground, he would demand a lawyer and let the Pashagora machine grind into action.

Later the next day, red and green lights twinkled on the helipad atop the Federal Building in Westwood as a Blackhawk lowered to the pad. It was still dark; dawn was a couple of hours away. Richardson and Harcourt turned aside from the downdraft of thrashed air. Within seconds, the blades began their wind-down, the door opened and three men exited, hunched in the usual manner of those running beneat whirling helicopter blades.

"We've got him at last," Richardson said to Harcourt, his words scattering away amidst the noise and clatter.

Mel's escorts handed him over to Harcourt and Robertson and returned to the waiting helicopter.

"Why were you returning to India with Ms. Keenan's computer, Mr. Pashagora?"

Mel took a deep breath. "We were to both go to Mumbai, but became separated."

"Separated? Whatever do you mean?" Harcourt asked, facing Mel, Richardson at his side, across the conference table that earlier sported Kate Keenan and crew.

"We were held up by two men in a truck. I managed to take away the man's gun, but they grabbed her into the vehicle and drove away," Mel said warily. "I would like to call my lawyer, if you don't mind."

"Where did this happen? Didn't she struggle? Didn't you try to save her?" continued Harcourt, ignoring the man's request.

"On Highway Five," Mel answered brusquely, "And I want my lawyer. I have a right to..."

"You didn't think to call the police?" Richardson asked.

"*I want to speak with my lawyer!*"

The agents exchanged glances. The government had the computer, and technically their work was complete. Someone else could take over if he was to going to lawyer up.

A. G. Hayes

Chapter 97

Vicky Vance had not spoken to Kumar Pashagora in years, and when she heard his voice on the phone, it turned her blood cold. Kumar was quick, simple and direct. He'd arranged his son's bail. He wanted his son back in India at once, and he ordered her to make it happen. Now.

Vicky Vance was used to deadlines, but also knew if Kumar's orders were not carried out, she'd likely be found dead. The queen of gossip and dark secrets weighed her chances and promptly decided it was time to retire. The internet was beating the hell out of her profession anyway.

"Lev, this is Vicky. Thank God you're at home."

"I was just leaving, Vicky. What's up?"

"It's about Mel."

Vicky hastily told him about the call from Pashagora.

"Where are you, Vicky?"

"At home. Can you come over?"

"Listen, Vicky, this is what I want you to do."

Lev turned to Kate, "You're not going to believe this. Vicky Vance is going to pick us up. An elderly woman driving alone and stopping momentarily to consult a road map won't be suspect. We'll be out the door and into her car in seconds."

"Why did she phone you?"

Lev told her and watched Kate's eyes widen by the second.

Normally, there was no way the notorious Vicky Vance would do another's bidding. Nevertheless, she was happy to drive over to Lev's house and pick him up as long as it included the possibility of saving her ass from the wrath of Kumar.

She drove from her home in Beverly Hills and headed up Laurel Canyon toward Lookout Mountain Avenue. It was already dark, and she had a hard time reading the names of the myriad streets that branched off Laurel Canyon. The further she drove up the winding gorge, the harder it became.

Finally, she pulled over, and not at Lev's house. She'd made a wrong turn somewhere. She cussed and muttered to herself as she rummaged for her cell phone.

"Lev, I can't find the way to your dammed house! I'm on a narrow road, trees all around me, not a street lamp in sight."

"What's the name of the street, Vicky?"

"I can't remember. I've been up and down so many damn twists and turns."

"Okay, Vicky. Calm down. Turn around and go back until you reach Laurel and find a street sign you can read. Then stop and call me again. I'll direct you from there."

Vicky was about launch into a tirade, when she remembered Kumar's orders. She needed Lev. "Right," she said and snapped her phone closed.

It took five minutes and about an inch of paint off the left fender to get her car turned around on the narrow road. Finally, back on Laurel Canyon, she got a bright idea. No way was she going to be driving those bloody footpaths these canyon dwellers called streets. She dialed Beverly Hills Cab.

Five minutes later, a cab pulled up behind her. Vicky got out of her car, locked it, walked to the cab and got in. "Two-one-three-three Lookout Mountain Avenue and step on it."

"A cab just pulled up outside, Lev," Kate said.

"Who in the devil?"

"It's Vicky," Kate exclaimed.

Lev opened the door as Vicky marched up the path.

"What are you doing? Lev, you and Kate follow me back to the cab and make it snappy. The meter's running."

Very little in the way of conversation was exchanged on the ride back to Vicky's car. Lev cast many an anxious glance through the cab's back window but there were no signs of a tail. Vicky paid the cab and the three of them quickly climbed into Vicky's car.

"Are you sure none of Kumar's people are trailing us, Lev?" There was a nervous edge to Vicky's voice.

"Not that I can see, Vicky." Lev was, however, certain

that the NSA were following somehow. Fox and Hounds. "Did Kumar say where Mel was, Vicky?"

"Yes, at Stella Rae's house."

Chapter 98

The two government technicians examining Kate's computer leapt back from their workbench. The screen suddenly went blank, the computer began hissing, and a pale greenish smoke with an acrid odor issued from within.

"What the hell?" a young man in a white lab coat cried.

The other tech, a young woman, stood petrified, fully aware of the consequences that would arise from the mishap. "It happened the moment you tried to extract the program."

Richardson got the news in his office and slammed down the phone. Fuming, he took the elevator to the basement of the Federal building. Two steel reinforced glass doors whooshed open as he entered. The two techs stood nervously beside the growing heap of melted metal and plastic that moments before was Kate Keenan's computer. Richardson waved a hand in front of his face, trying to rid the terrible smell of burning printed circuitry. One of the techs handed him a wetted paper towel to place over his nose and mouth.

"What happened? How long is this going to take to repair?"

"Sir, there's no possibility of repair. This computer is totaled."

"No chance of repair? Totaled?" Richardson roared. "There has to be a way! This piece of equipment has national security preferential treatment clearance, do you understand?" What was left of the laptop lid suddenly fell backwards and dropped off.

At the moment the smoking lid toppled, Kate, Lev and Vicky were entering Stella Rae's home. Lev had contacted Ethan and Stacy, given them his location, brought them up to date, told them to park on the street, a car facing each way, and instructed them to call if anything suspicious, like an unmarked vehicle with government plates, showed up.

Stella was sober. However, she had a drink in one hand as she led Kate, Lev and Vicky into the living room.

"Where's that Sonofabitch?" Lev growled, scouring the room with a glare that would have melted iron. He wanted to wring Mel's neck. No one hauled a client out of his office with a letter opener pointed at the jugular. No one!

Stella pointed upward, "In the master bedroom. He's armed and has locked himself inside. He won't come out until Vicky presents him with an acceptable plan to move him out of the country."

"I can get him back to India. I'll have the swine deported!" Kate fumed.

"Stop! Everyone!" Vicky's trumpet voice took over. "Remember, I'm the hostage here. If I don't get that bastard back to India, Kumar will…"

"Vicky's right," Lev soothed. "Mel is waiting to be escorted out of this house for a safe trip to India, and he's expecting you to make it happen."

"Why did Kumar choose you, Vicky? What connection does he have with you?" Kate asked.

Vicky slumped into an easy chair, her face, usually perfect, was in need of repair. "Blackmail." Her voice cracked with emotion as she spoke the word. "I became part of Kumar's world several years ago. I've been passing him inside information on anything to do with Hollywood for years."

Stella drained her drink. "'Spy' would be a better word, Vicky. That's what we've all been at one time or another. Mel, myself and God knows how many others. We were all tools."

"I need a drink," Vicky said.

Stella refilled her own glass and then poured vodka for Vicky. "Start drinking and thinking, old lady."

The image of Vicky Vance disheveled and tired, clutching a glass of vodka in a shaky hand, acutely aware of the errors of her past caused Kate to pause. Her program to change the face of Hollywood had a darker side that could possibility bite her, too, one day.

Lev broke the silence. "Well, Vicky, what's it going to be?"

"I don't know what to do, Lev." Her chin dropped to her

chest and the glass fell from her fingers. Sobbing uncontrollably, she said, "For the first time in years, I don't know what to do."

Kate stared at the glass. It hadn't broken. It lay on the thick carpet, its contents soaking into the pile. Crouching in front of Vicky, Kate took the woman's scrawny hand in hers and looked up at Lev. "I think it's time we called Harcourt."

The tableau presented a tragic spectacle to Lev. He watched as Vicky Vance, the Sovereign of Scandal, whose words, even in these times of 'anything goes' could ruin those who dared not to bend a knee at her every whim, crumpled, her sovereignty ended.

Kate picked up the glass and placed it on a side table. "Lev, call Stace and Dad here. We should be together when Harcourt and the others arrive."

"Okay, I'll phone them, and Harcourt immediately afterwards."

Stella refreshed her drink and sipped twice before asking, "What about Mel?"

"He stays in the bedroom for now, Stella," Lev replied.

Mel had listened intently to every word spoken in the living room from the moment Vicky, Lev and Kate entered. It had taken all his money and savoir-faire, but he'd eventually persuaded Stella to leave on the wireless intercom between the bedroom and living room.

Chapter 99

Richardson phone-contacted Harcourt about the self-destruction of Kate's computer, moving Kate immediately back in Harcourt's cross hairs.

"That little witch bugged the computer to blow, Richardson concluded.

"Where is she now?"

"Leventhal's place. I have two men parked up the street on Lookout Mountain Avenue—no cars have been in or out. A cab dropped someone at the entrance and drove away, that's it."

"Fine, I'll pick her up and bring her here." Harcourt hung up.

Harcourt's phone trilled immediately. It was Lev.

"Where are you, Leventhal?"

Lev told him that he, Kate and several others were at Stella Rae's with Mel locked in the bedroom.

As he listened, Harcourt's jaw torqued. After the explanation, he brusquely ordered Lev and the others to remain where they were until he arrived. *So much for being Master of the Hounds,* he thought ironically.

"Harcourt's on the way," Lev said lowering into a leather

easy chair. Ethan and Stace beat Harcourt to Stella Rae's house by five minutes.

Mel reacted to Lev's words at once. He had no intention of falling into the hands of the Feds again.

The master bedroom, in the back part of the large house, overlooked a garden of trees and bushes. Switching off the bedroom lights, Mel went to the window, slid it open and stuck his head out. Ten feet below, the edge of the patio roof jutted out into the yard. Stuffing the 9-millimeter Beretta his 'Pashagora owned' lawyer had left him into his waist band, Mel eased out of the window and nimbly lowered himself to the top of the patio.

Within seconds, he was across the back lawn, over a redwood fence, and into a neighbor's yard. Thankfully, there were no barking dogs with which to contend.

Vicky slopped vodka into her empty glass with a shaky hand. "Lev, I'm going to tell all I know about Pashagora's criminal intrusion into the workings of Hollywood and seek protection under the government's Witness Protection Program."

Lev and Stace murmured approval.

"What are you going to tell them, Kate?" Ethan asked.

"Well, Dad, assuming they've gotten hold of my computer and have unsuccessfully tried to copy the program off of it, they're most likely going to want to haul my ass back to the

Federal building."

"If they've lost the computer, you're all that's left, Kate," Lev said.

"Okay, you're my agent. What do you think I should say, Lev?"

"Why not cut a deal?" Ethan cut in softly. "Sell the Feds the program. You own the patents; you could negotiate for millions. Think about it, Baby. If the program fell into movie industry hands, Hollywood could end up the same as the steel mills did in Pennsylvania with thousands out of work. The mills never made it back and neither would Hollywood."

"Yeah, Dad, you're right. I've been thinking about that. Director John Landis was right about Corporate Hollywood searching relentlessly for a way to make movies without the cost and headaches of stars, crews and directors, but I don't think it's ready for my program."

"They're here," Stella whispered, peeking through parted curtains as the doorbell chimed.

"I'll get it." Kate went into the hall and opened the front door. "Good evening, Agent Harcourt. Do come in. You're in luck. Two of the ladies you said you were interested in inter-viewing are here."

Harcourt and two agents followed Kate into the living room. He took in the occupants with a sweeping glance. A drowsy-eyed young woman with a red rose tattooed on her shoulder was draped in a chair. A blotchy faced old woman stared up at him over the top of her tilting cocktail glass. The others in the room, he knew already.

Kate indicated Vicky. "Ms. Vicky Vance," Then Stella. "Ms. Stella Rae."

"Good evening, ladies. I have a few questions before Miz Keenan and I return to the Federal building," Harcourt announced.

"I know everything about the Pashagora cartel," Vicky blurted out, rising half out of her chair. "You have to put me into a protection program! They're going to kill me!"

Chapter 100

Vicky Vance and her lawyer sat in the conference room at the Federal building. Vicky was talking. Harcourt, Richardson, the tight-faced middle-aged woman and Falk were silent, listening.

A change had come over Vicky. She sat relaxed; the knowledge she was safe inside the Federal building had eased her fears.

"Getting involved with criminals was a damn silly thing to do. Becoming involved with Pashagora and his gang was beyond stupidity. Nonetheless, I did. At first, it was easy. They made me feel important, saying I was the best reporter in Hollywood and that I could be useful to Bollywood." She smiled, adding as postscript, "It's a common ailment in Hollywood, believing your own publicity." Vicky turned to her lawyer; they spoke briefly, and at his nod she continued. "Does the name Abul Abu Gulshan mean anything to you?" she asked.

The trio looked at each other. Falk sat straight up, but remained in the role of an observer. He watched Kate closely. The middle-aged woman said the name was familiar, but to continue with her story.

"Run his name through your computers and see what pops up. It could save me a lot of talking," Vicky shot back.

The woman gave a 'do it' nod to Richardson, who pushed away from the table and left the room. The middle-aged woman taking the deposition leaned forward, recorded the time of Richardson's exit and announced a short intermission. Fifteen minutes later, Richardson was sitting in his office behind his desk, stern faced, hands clasped together, elbows on a leather edged blotter. Kate sat across from him. Harcourt stood behind Richardson. Falk was sitting quietly in a corner.

"Miz Keenan. Listen to me carefully." Richardson nodded to Harcourt who switched on the tape recorder and announced time, place and occupants. Kate surveyed the room's occupants and stared at Falk, her eyes sharpening.

Looking down at a piece of paper as if reading it aloud, the continued: "Vicky Vance has given us some startling facts and a name of interest, which, in conjunction with the recent attempts to kidnap you and steal your computer program have our government even more deeply concerned. Abul Abu Gulshan is one of Interpol's most wanted. A central figure in organized crime in India and Asia, he's also a prime suspect in the nineteen-thirty-three Mumbai serial explosion case that ripped through the city killing two hundred and fifty-seven innocent people, injuring over seven hundred more. Kumar Pashagora is the nominal head of the India cartel overseen by

Abul Abu Gulshan."

Richardson glanced up from the paper and glanced at Falk, who nodded, as if already familiar with everything Richardson had said. "The cartel is operated out of Europe. Gulshan's *forte* is extortion, and with Pashagora's assistance, it is rife throughout the Indian film industry. Most producers and directors have had to interact indirectly with this man, who ultimately demands the overseas rights of their films in return for 'protection' during production and 'insurance' during post-production. Gulshan, we believe, was involved in the murder of business Tycoon Rajesh Rocha, the killing of actor Manisha Koirala's secretary, and the attempted murder of film producer Pradeep Jain."

Richardson paused, glancing up again. "These names meant little to us here in California. Nonetheless, given what we now know, as Agent Harcourt suggested earlier, you would be well advised to consider our offer of protection."

"Where does Mel fit into all this?" Kate asked, staring at Falk, recognizing at last where the real power was within the room.

"At this point we have no idea. When we have him in custody, he'll be interrogated, then most likely deported back to India."

Richardson pushed aside his fact sheet, glanced again at Falk, and leaned forward. "I've been authorized by our government to make you part of our Secure National Twenty-one Black Ops computer network at NSA—top security clearance, a generous fee for the 'purchase' of your system, plus a well-paying government job."

"And if I accepted this offer, you could use my program any way the government saw fit and I'd have no way to stop you. Correct?"

Before Richardson could nod his agreement, Kate held up a hand and spoke directly to Falk. "The offer is enticing, and working for NSA could indeed prove interesting. Still, I must make a decision, and knowing my program has potential for military use, as a good citizen, I have no wish to stop the program getting to the DOD as soon as possible."

Harcourt and Robinson brightened somewhat. Falk remained neutral, his eyes, like a laser, boring into her.

Kate reclined in her chair and stared at the ceiling. "My Dad and I have decided my program could be more of a hindrance than help to Hollywood. Too many people would lose their jobs, and the economy being what it is right now, well, I'd hate to be responsible for turning Hollywood into a ghost town."

Harcourt and Richardson bent forward, eager to hear her decision. Falk remained relaxed and focused on Kate.

"However, I would prefer to continue my work in private with an organization within the government that might allow me more autonomy," Kate said to Falk, who gave a small smile.

Richardson jumped to his feet. "You can't do that!"

"I'm sure there's some agency within the government other than NSA that would be interested in my work and could meet all the terms of your offer, Agent Richardson," Kate said, staring into Agent Richardson's eyes, but speaking as if talking to Falk.

Kate continued to stare at a dumbfounded Richardson and Harcourt.

Satisfied she'd correctly voiced her counteroffer, Kate redirected everyone's attention to a second issue that was of personal concern. "Is my friend Vicky Vance going to be safe? You will be arranging something for her along with her new identity, say in communication, I'm sure, won't you?" Without waiting for an answer, Kate rose to her feet and smiled wryly. "Vicky will be sorely missed in Hollywood."

A. G. Hayes

Chapter 101

The next few days were hectic.

"Your experiences since the wrap party, Kate, lead me to believe you'd be a gift to the NSA," Lev said quietly. Joanie and Stacy were sitting on a plump settee in Kate's living room, Ethan comfortably between them.

Lev and Kate relaxed in twin beige easy chairs facing Joanie, Ethan and Stacy.

Stacy took a sip of her wine. "Are you nuts, Lev? They'd take her program and have Kate sitting behind a desk eight hours a day doing some humdrum office job."

"Sitting in an office all day, at best, managing other people" said Joanie. "It's out of character and would be a terrible waste of your scientific, programming and writing talents."

Ethan exchanged a grin with Lev. "Lev's not crazy, Stace. He and I felt it might be a good idea if Kate worked for NSA, or, better yet, the Defense Advanced Research Program Agency, DARPA, or maybe the Defense Intelligence Agency, DIA."

"Dad, we've already discussed this at length. I've already assured you that I'd run my decision past you guys before committing to it. And I've come up with one I think would work for me."

Everyone perked up.

Stace nodded. "Tell us more, Kate."

"Well, NSA offered to 'buy' my program. I've already advised them that I will talk with my patent and business attornys and get back to them."

"I meant about DARPA. Or the DIA. I don't see you in either an office," Stace said.

"NSA offered to introduce me to them as well as several other agencies within the government. If one suits me, then they'll train me. After that, I'd be back here in Hollywood, doing what I've wanted to do before all this blew up: writing. Given all I've experienced, I've a particularly good thriller screenplay in my head that, with some adjustments for national security, I'd like to see brought to the silver screen. Megastar studios, at NSA's encouragement, has already agreed to option them and pay me an advance even before I put it on paper. After my 'agency' training, I'd be consulted on a 'need to help' basis."

"By 'agency' you mean DARPA or DIA?" Stace asked.

Kate smiled. "Not exactly. I'm not really at liberty to say." Kate had figured out that Agent Falk worked for a 'special' agency, as the head of the agency had put it "in association with various government agencies." The biggest attraction, however, was Falk. She wanted to see more of him. She felt his authority, his piercing intelligence and a connection with him that she was hoping was reciprocated.

"Of course, we understand. Well, it all sounds very intriguing," Stacy said, disappointed not to hear the details.

"As I said, whatever agency she finally chooses to work with, it'll be Kate's decision. Either way, I'll still have my star client."

"Anything new on Mel's whereabouts?" Stacy asked, attempting to change the subject away from what seemed to her like Kate's possible excursion into the dark world of cloaks and daggers.

"Not a word," Lev said. "I'll give Harcourt a call in the morning, but I don't expect he'll tell us even if he knows. He was glad to see the end of us."

A. G. Hayes

Chapter 102

Pradeep Kurade, the government asset with an office on Cuffe Parade, Mumbai, placed a coded call by satellite phone to his contact in Washington, reporting that Melhi Pashagora had definitely arrived back at his home in Mumbai. Since then, no one had seen or heard from him.

A. G. Hayes

Chapter 103

Hank and Jilly sailed into Marina Costa Baja shortly before darkness and tied up at an overnight courtesy mooring. Hank checked in with the dock master, booked a three-day mooring and inquired about the best yacht broker in the area.

Back on board, Hank related to Jilly the results of his inquiries as she fried eggs on the galley stove. "I go see a man named José Gutierrez in the morning. He's supposed to be the best ship broker around."

Jilly grunted, flipped the eggs over easy and slid them onto a plate. "I hope they have a decent store. God, I'm tired of fry-ups."

Hank dipped a crust of bread into a yoke and agreed. "The dock master said this José guy he is trustworthy and has rich clients, as well as a seaworthy inventory to choose from, should we decide to do an exchange."

"They all say that, Hank. I vote we sell the boat, get off the ocean, fly away someplace safe and drop out of sight."

Hank finished his eggs and leaned back. "Maybe you're right. I'll definitely see what I can get for the yacht. Remember when I told you about the sale of the company and the bank transactions?"

Jilly nodded, "Yes, of course."

"Well, I got a call from a man who has a business not dissimilar to TolomeoTechnics. He'd heard I was selling my business, and, hearing it had already sold, asked if I'd be interested in buying in with him. I said I'd get back to him."

"You told me the transaction wouldn't be known until after we arrived in India."

"I said it wouldn't become *public*. There's always a few who hear of things before they become public."

"You'd leave a trail a mile wide if you went back into business now, Hank."

"I don't think so. His plant is in Wales."

Jilly looked surprised, "Wales as in Welsh?"

"Lovely country, Jilly. We could have a house there and another place in London. Make up a legend. No one would know or care who we were. I'd be the silent partner. It's mostly my contacts he needs."

Jilly, always one to make up her mind quickly, leaned across the galley table and kissed Hank on the forehead.

"Sell the yacht, call your friend, and let's go to Wales."

Chapter 104

It was early June when Kate returned to Hollywood. Lev and Ethan met her at LAX and updated each other as Lev drove her to her home on North Switzer Avenue.

"It's good to be back in my own place," Kate said tossing her carryon onto the couch and slumping into one of the easy chairs.

"It's good to have you home, Baby," Ethan said. "Stace would have come with us to pick you up, but was busy at the office."

"Your few emails sounded like you were enjoying your training," Lev chimed.

"They kept us very busy."

"Will you have to go back, or are you assigned to a local office?"

"Just like they said, Dad, I'm free to do as I please until they call me on a 'consultation' or give me a permanent assignment. Could be a day or a year. Who knows." She grinned. "For now, I'll be working from home, later from wherever they send me. And that's all I can tell you."

"Sounds like a dream job," Ethan said. "Now I have some news for you, Baby: Stace and I are getting married. We haven't set a date yet, but it'll be before the end of the year."

Kate jumped up and flung her arms around Ethan's neck. "Oh, I'm so happy for you, Dad! You'll make a great couple."

"Lev will be best man and we'd like you and Joanie to be maids of honor."

"A church wedding!" Kate exclaimed. "Who's giving the bride away?"

"Stace has an uncle who lives in Denver. He's all the family she has now."

"I can't believe this. It's such a surprise."

"Stace and your Dad knew each other years ago," Lev said. "They lost touch after he left town. Things rekindled since they met up again after our trip to Nevada."

"We should celebrate. Any wine in the house? I want to make a toast." Kate, suddenly in wedding mode, was bubbling over with excitement.

Ethan, who had been house sitting while Kate was away, answered. "There's a bottle of Chablis cooling in the refrigerator. Will that do?"

The bottle was half-empty when Kate asked, "Which church did you two pick?"

Lev and Ethan exchanged glances before Ethan answered, "The Wee Kirk O' The Heather in Forest Lawn, Glendale."

Lev saw Kate's eyes widen with surprise. "They match and dispatch at Forest Lawn, Kate," he explained with a smile.

"Yes, well, I know. It's just that…"

Ethan reached out and grasped Kate's hand. "Stace loves that little church. Her mother and father were married there. She used to visit it often, and sit and enjoy the peace and quiet. She wants something beautiful to happen there again, to erase the horrible memory of what occurred there a few months ago.

A. G. Hayes

Chapter 105

Toward the end of August, Kate had finished outlining her screenplay, tentatively called, "Charlotte's Webpage," a story of a woman and a man who vanished while sailing their yacht in the Pacific.

The chime of an incoming email made her pause. Clicking to her incoming box, she read the message: "Contact us by agreed method. We have need to know concerning a major breakthrough in robotics. You will be working from the London Office. Details to follow."

Kate, as she learned during her training, permanently erased the message and sat quietly at her desk knowing that Hank Tolomeo and Jilly Suede were no longer missing at sea as the "major breakthrough in robotics" had the former TolomeoTechnics written all over it.

The assignment would require a rewrite of "Charlotte's Webpage." But first the assignment, then the rewrite.

If you enjoyed *Finding Kate* consider the first book in the Koski and Falk series, *Who's Killing All the Lawyers?*

Lawyers are being murdered by laser-driven arrows. The FBI believes that someone is training Native Americans to take over the US economic system. Joe Falk and Susan Koski are assigned to find the hired killer and The Fox, the real force behind the killings.

GREAT SOUTHWEST BOOK FESTIVAL AWARD

AMAZON KINDLE GENRE BESTSELLER

…the second in the Koski and Falk series, *The Judas List:*

A 700-year-old prayer book, a key and a faded blueprint came to light and begin a search for Nazi Herman Goering's treasure. In modern day Vienna, American agents Koski and Falk must locate the treasure and the Judas List—a compendium of individuals and organizations that financed WWII, and intend to bring about the Fourth Reich.
PACIFIC RIM BOOK FESTIVAL AWARD

…the third book in the Falk and Koski adventure series, *Imminent Danger* by A. G. Hayes.

Jamul, an adored American pop singer, dreams of a grand show of Islamic Jihad power, intending to use a biological weapon to eradicate religious leaders at an Easter service at the Hollywood Bowl. Cerberus agents Joe Falk and Susan Koski must stop the next brutal terrorist attack on American soil.

LA BOOK FESTIVAL AWARD

…the fourth in the multi-award-winning Koski and Falk series, *The Chemical Factor*:

A stolen weapon of mass destruction hidden years ago on board the Queen Mary has remained there undisturbed. Up to now. Agents Falk and Koski are called in to evacuate the ship and somehow locate the bomb. Risking their lives to locate the weapon, they discover that a Girl Scout has strayed from her group during evacuation and is hiding in the ship.

PACIFIC RIM BOOK FESTIVAL AWARD

…and the fifth in the multi-award-winning Koski and Falk series, *Quantum Death*:

Koski and Falk come up against what very well may prove to be their most complex and dangerous case yet: The Quantum Death Machine. Each faces mortal peril, while, at the same time, their smoldering relationship begins to heat up.

About the Author

A. G. Hayes studied television writing at UCLA. He has published short fiction for CBS TV and other television production companies. He lives in the Sierra Nevada Foothills and spends his time writing and traveling to nearly every part of the world. He has used personal experiences gained during service with the British intelligence in Eastern Europe and the Middle East to enrich the characters of his protagonist teams. He is the multi-award-winning author of *Who's Killing All the Lawyers* (Savant 2011), *The Judas List* (Savant 2012), *Imminent Danger* (Savant 2013), *The Chemical Factor* (Savant 2015) and *Quantum Death* (Savant 2016).

A. G. Hayes

If you enjoyed *Finding Kate,* consider these other fine books from Savant Books and Publications:

Essay, Essay, Essay by Yasuo Kobachi
Aloha from Coffee Island by Walter Miyanari
Footprints, Smiles and Little White Lies by Daniel S. Janik
The Illustrated Middle Earth by Daniel S. Janik
Last and Final Harvest by Daniel S. Janik
A Whale's Tale by Daniel S. Janik
Tropic of California by R. Page Kaufman
Tropic of California (the companion music CD) by R. Page Kaufman
The Village Curtain by Tony Tame
Dare to Love in Oz by William Maltese
The Interzone by Tatsuyuki Kobayashi
Today I Am a Man by Larry Rodness
The Bahrain Conspiracy by Bentley Gates
Called Home by Gloria Schumann
Kanaka Blues by Mike Farris
First Breath edited by Z. M. Oliver
Poor Rich by Jean Blasiar
Ammon's Horn by Guerrino Amati
The Jumper Chronicles by W. C. Peever
William Maltese's Flicker by William Maltese
My Unborn Child by Orest Stocco
Last Song of the Whales by Four Arrows
Perilous Panacea by Ronald Klueh
Falling but Fulfilled by Zachary M. Oliver
Mythical Voyage by Robin Ymer
Hello, Norma Jean by Sue Dolleris
Richer by Jean Blasiar
Manifest Intent by Mike Farris
Charlie No Face by David B. Seaburn
Number One Bestseller by Brian Morley
My Two Wives and Three Husbands by S. Stanley Gordon
In Dire Straits by Jim Currie
Wretched Land by Mila Komarnisky
Chan Kim by Ilan Herman
Who's Killing All the Lawyers? by A. G. Hayes
Ammon's Horn by G. Amati
Wavelengths edited by Zachary M. Oliver
Almost Paradise by Laurie Hanan
Communion by Jean Blasiar and Jonathan Marcantoni
The Oil Man by Leon Puissegur
Random Views of Asia from the Mid-Pacific by William E. Sharp
The Isla Vista Crucible by Reilly Ridgell

Finding Kate

Blood Money by Scott Mastro
In the Himalayan Nights by Anoop Chandola
On My Behalf by Helen Doan
Traveler's Rest by Jonathan Marcantoni
Keys in the River by Tendai Mwanaka
Chimney Bluffs by David B. Seaburn
The Loons by Sue Dolleris
Light Surfer by David Allan Williams
The Judas List by A. G. Hayes
Path of the Templar - Book 2 of The Jumper Chronicles by W. C. Peever
The Desperate Cycle by Tony Tame
Shutterbug by Buz Sawyer
Blessed are the Peacekeepers by Tom Donnelly/Mike Munger
Purple Haze by George B. Hudson
The Turtle Dances by Daniel S. Janik
The Lazarus Conspiracies by Richard Rose
Imminent Danger by A. G. Hayes
Lullaby Moon by Malia Elliott of Leon & Malia
Volutions edited by Suzanne Langford
In the Eyes of the Son by Hans Brinckmann
The Hanging of Dr. Hanson by Bentley Gates
Written in the Stars - An Anthology edited by Sabrina Favors
Elaine of Corbenic by Tima Z. Newman
Ballerina Birdies by Marina Yamamoto
More, More Time by David Seaburn
Crazy Like Me by Erin Lee
Cleopatra Unconquered by Helen R. Davis
Valedictory by Daniel Scott
The Chemical Factor by A. G. Hayes
Running From the Pack edited by Helen R. Davis
Big Heaven by Charlotte Hebert
All Things Await by Seth Clabough
Captain Riddle's Treasure by GV Rama Rao
Libido Tsunami by Cate Burns

Coming Works
The Adventures of Purple Head, Buddha Monkey Sticky Feet by Erik Bracht
Cereus by Z. Roux
In the Shadows of My Mind by Andrew Massie

http://www.savantbooksandpublications.com